About th

I am a former primary school teacher from Rochdale whose passion and speciality was promoting imaginative writing, with an emphasis placed firmly on the joy of the written word, for ten- and eleven-year-old children.

Horror in the Dells is the product of the stimulus I provided pupils with during my time in years five and six. To create the setting for this story, I would take my class into the adjacent dells and once there we would create a fantasy world of witches, goblins and other gruesome creatures which fired the children's imaginations and expanded their vocabulary, the end product of which was the creation of some wonderful writing, which they were invariably proud of.

My other novellas are based on stories I created to use as starting points in order to excite pupils' imaginations and stimulate an enthusiasm to not only write, but to enjoy the experience.

My other passion involves an interest in the evolution of recreation in the nineteenth century on which I wrote a thesis to successfully gain a PhD from Manchester University.

HORROR IN THE DELLS

Stuart Barlow

HORROR IN THE DELLS

Vanguard Press

A CIP catalogue record for this title is
available from the British Library.

ISBN 978-1-80016-596-0

*Vanguard Press is an imprint of
Pegasus Elliot Mackenzie Publishers Ltd.*
www.pegasuspublishers.com

First Published in 2022

**Vanguard Press
Sheraton House Castle Park
Cambridge England**

Printed & Bound in Great Britain

Dedication

Dedicated to all those children who entered the Dells and survived to write a horror story!

Introduction

The date was the 31st of October. The school bell rang with its usual clatter to signify dinner time at Ratchcombe Primary School. Year 6 were about to enter the dining hall excited and noisy, a state of mind which had little to do with the thought of the food they were about to eat, but everything to do with the stimulating lesson they had just experienced. They had just returned from a visit to the dells, a densely wooded, neglected, and in many ways intimidating, part of Denebrook Park which formed a boundary around one part of the school grounds.

The class had gone there with their teacher, Ms Salmon, to explore and experience the exciting environment as part of the stimulus for writing a horror story entitled 'Horror in the Dells'. The aim of the lesson had been to ignite the children's imagination by enabling them to experience a place that provided a rich setting for a horror story based on the weird and terrifying happenings, that, rumour had it, occurred on the 'Night of All Hallows' in Denebrook Park, an area renowned for witchcraft and evil spells, or so their mischievous teacher informed them, before, during and after the spine-tingling excursion into the desolate, wooded dells.

As the class had wandered through the dells, Ms

Salmon stimulated her pupils' fertile imaginations with graphic images of werewolves howling, teeth-gnashing ghouls floating through the air; hobgoblins lurking behind every bush; animated trees with skeletal fingers clawing unwanted visitors; squirrels that could speak; worst of all *witches*: grotesque caricatures of human beings, intent only on practising their wicked magic on unsuspecting visitors to the dells, with an especial taste for inquisitive children!

How the children lapped it up, frightening each other with ever more ghastly and terrifying scenarios. Behind every tree, under the bushes, lurked a nasty creature in their mind's eye. By the time they returned to the classroom the children were excited and ready to write a horror story like no other. Their imaginations were on fire!

For Kelly and Sophie, it had been scary enough visiting the dells in daylight hours. Like the rest of the class they had been excited, but also frightened by the dells experience and had kept close to Jess, their protector, though she didn't see it that way. She, like Richard and Andrew and the rest of the class, had enjoyed battling their way through the dense, often painful undergrowth where brambles grabbed their clothes and scratched their legs and hands. They slipped on the muddy paths, sliding down wet slopes, whilst being bombarded with tales of evil witches and wicked hobgoblins that frequented the dells on one occasion only: on All Hallows' Eve, which was that very night!

On their return to the classroom, the group of friends

were excited and talkative.

"That was scary," said Sophie, biting her nails.

"I'm still shivering, but not because of the cold," said Kelly.

"That was fantastic!" exclaimed Andrew, excited.

"Terrific," added Richard.

"I can't wait to go back," announced Jess, enthusiastically.

"If only all those hideous creatures were real," said Kelly, foolishly.

"I want to meet a goblin," said Sophie, "and shake his hand."

"I want a conversation with a talking squirrel," said Kelly.

"I'd like to see a werewolf," said Andrew, "in a dangerous sort of way."

"I don't believe in witches," said Jess, defiantly. "They don't exist, except in the eyes of weak-minded children," she added, looking directly at Kelly and Sophie, who looked away, pretending not to hear.

Ms Salmon interrupted their discussion. "All right class 6, I can see you are all dying to start writing your story, but before you do I have to tell you that the supernatural events that are rumoured to take place in the dells only occur on a leap year."

The class was more enthralled.

"Every leap year?" asked Andrew.

"No not every four years, just once in a generation."

"When is the next time it's likely to happen?" Andrew

persisted.

Ms Salmon thought for a moment and then said, "I think it could be this year!"

"How do you know it's going to happen?" asked Jess.

"Well the appearance of a strangely shaped plume of smoke emerging from the depths of the dells is a sign that something unusual, often sinister, is going to happen. Interestingly not everyone can see it. It's rumoured that you have got to possess special powers of observation," she added with a barely perceptible smile creasing her kind face.

As it was dinner time, the children left the classroom excited and intrigued, particularly the 'Super Sleuths' [Andrew, Richard, Jess, Sophie and Kelly].

"How fascinating," said Andrew.

"I wonder if it really is this year," said Sophie, shivering slightly.

Ms Salmon, who had followed them out of the classroom, overheard her.

"If it is you mustn't go anywhere near the dells at night or you might be turned into a toad or something worse," she said with a smile.

"Or put into a cauldron and boiled and then eaten," suggested Scott who had been lurking behind them.

The others smiled, but Kelly didn't. She glared at the boy, her enemy.

Ms Salmon intervened to prevent an argument, or worse. "Thank you Scott, that will do. Now, this afternoon you can all plan your stories. We've already looked at the success criteria and brainstormed the vocabulary and then you can write the most exciting stories of your time in my class."

As the group headed to the dining hall, an excited Jess said, "We've got to investigate the dells tonight to see if this really is that special year."

"It could be true," said Andrew, "weird people have been rumoured to exist from the beginning of time. But there is very little evidence of witchcraft."

Jess and Richard smiled at one another. They really couldn't resist the thought of a nocturnal investigation, despite the potential dangers. The other three gathered round.

"It's agreed then. We'll visit the dells tonight and see if any of this nonsense is actually true," said Richard, thinking that it was all the product of his teacher's fertile imagination, despite what she had said; a remark he was to regret many times over as it unleashed a series of events that would endanger all their lives!

Not knowing this, they all nodded, though some less enthusiastically than others.

Chapter 1

The Super Sleuth Club members were grouped together in the dinner hall, excited by their experience in the dells and overflowing with ideas for their stories which they expressed loudly, much to the annoyance of the two dinner ladies called Mrs Dumpling and Mrs Sour. The ladies had taken a dislike to this particular group of children, considering them to be too talkative and too happy. School, especially the dining hall, was a place to be endured not enjoyed!

"I'm going to write about witches in my story. Horrible, nasty witches, who turn people into toads!" squealed Sophie, glancing at the dinner ladies.

"My witch is going to have a magic wand and grant me three wishes," announced Kelly, waving an imaginary wand above her head, accidently striking Mrs Dumpling (who had sidled up to the group unnoticed to listen in to their conversation to see if she could get them into trouble) on her bulbous nose.

She recoiled in horror clutching her face, trying to stem the imaginary flow of blood.

"You little monster!" she screamed advancing towards the startled Kelly, with malice in her eyes and a serving spoon in her hand which she intended to use as a weapon to hammer home a message to the distraught girl.

"I'm sorry," Kelly muttered, backing away from the fearsome dinner lady not seeing, but colliding with, Mrs Sour, who was in the process of carrying a tray of uneaten food back to the slop bucket, and sending her tumbling to the floor where she was joined by the contents of the discarded meal, a sloppy lasagne. This did little to improve the already filthy state of the apron she was wearing, or the expression on her miserable face.

"Now look what you've done," shouted Mrs Dumpling releasing the spoon from her grasp, which landed neatly, and painfully, on a small boy's head with such force that he was sure he heard the bell ring. He dashed back to his classroom, clutching his sore skull, thinking dinner time was over. As he was doing so, Mrs Dumpling strode up to Kelly and Sophie, pushed them aside and helped Mrs Sour, dripping with disgorged meat and pasta and spitting venom and lasagne, to her feet.

"Who did that?" she bawled, scraping the food from her eyes and wiping her hands on the hair and face of a girl who was enjoying her lunch. That is, until the dripping fingers of the enraged dinner lady entered her nostrils, with considerable force.

"I can't see or breathe," the girl complained.

"Shut up. Stop complaining about something and nothing and eat your dinner!" screamed Mrs Dumpling, helping the child to do so by the expedient method of pushing her face into the bowl of soup she was no longer enjoying.

The angry dinner ladies were joined by their colleague, Mrs Onion, who hovered menacingly over the weeping Kelly and was about to dish out some rough justice when Jess intervened.

"Leave her alone," she said, bristling with indignation.

"It was clearly an accident," added Andrew.

"Unlike your actions," continued Richard.

"Well!" said Mrs Sour, through the curtain of gravy that continued to drip down her face. "I never."

"What cheek!" exclaimed Mrs Dumpling, appalled.

"Disgusting, I say. No manners, these brats. None at all," pronounced Mrs Salad. "Just look what you've done to Mrs Sour."

They did, and secretly enjoyed what they saw, though they didn't say so.

"She did it deliberately," growled Mrs Dumpling, and was about to grab the distraught Kelly when the children's teacher appeared. In the eyes of the three dinner ladies, Ms Salmon was far too soft with her pupils in general, but especially so with this group of know-it-alls, whom they particularly detested. Looking at the expressions on the faces of both children and dinner ladies the teacher quickly assessed the nature of the problem and intervened.

"Oh dear, Mrs Sour, you've obviously had an unfortunate accident."

The aggrieved lady was about to respond to the contrary when Ms Salmon continued.

"I suggest you get yourself cleaned up."

"But... bu..."

"I think you should do that before you distribute the remnants of the dinner that's covering most of your face onto more pupils."

Mrs Sour was appalled by this, what she considered to be a rude and inappropriate intervention by the teacher. This was dinner time; she and her colleagues were supposed to be in sole charge of proceedings. She peered across through her partially closed eyes at her two angry colleagues who, of course, shared her indignant views; teachers and children should know their place at dinner time and listen to the people who knew what they were doing, in other words them! But Ms Salmon wasn't finished.

"I think some children need your help," she said, pointing to a child whose head was resting in a soup bowl. "She appears to be choking."

Their faces turned crimson and hatred blazed from the eyes of all three dinner ladies. Mrs Dumpling dragged the girl's head out of the bowl by her hair as Mrs Sour stormed off towards the toilets to clean herself up. Muttering to themselves, Mrs Dumpling and Mrs Salad reluctantly moved away from the group and their teacher and shouted at nearby pupils who had been enjoying their lunch and the slapstick action until the vindictive dinner ladies directed their fury at them.

"I'll send you to head if you don't stop doing that," boomed Mrs Dumpling to a boy who had been foolish enough to allow a smile to enliven his cheeks.

Ms Salmon beamed at her pupils, knowing they were

excited by the story stimulus she had given them and left the dining hall with metaphorical daggers sticking in her back, dispatched by the disaffected women. Andrew, Richard and Jess shrugged their shoulders. Nothing the dinner ladies did surprised them, not yet! They lined up at the serving hatch and received their suspiciously small dinners and sat down together at a vacant table where they were shortly after joined by Sophie and a still upset Kelly.

Scott, who had observed Kelly's accident approached them. "Well done," he laughed, patting her on the back. "That was almost as enjoyable, though in a different way, as our visit to the dells. Do you think your accident was the result of a witch's spell?" he giggled.

Scott was a constant thorn in Kelly's side; they were always bickering. She threw her chair backwards as she got to her feet and was about to return Scott's gentle tap with more than a little interest, in the form of a full-blooded slap, when she was prevented from doing so firstly by Jess and then by the commotion that had developed behind her. This had come about because the chair Kelly discarded had thumped into the leg of the eavesdropping Mrs Sour who had returned to spy on them. She shrieked and collapsed onto the ground, apparently in agony, clutching her injured leg.

"You, you…" she garbled, pointing at the unfortunate Kelly.

"But it was an—"

"No it wasn't. You attacked poor Mrs Sour again, this time with a weapon!" screamed Mrs Dumpling, who had also returned. You're going to the head, and you'll be expelled for viciously attacking three innocent, kind hearted dinner ladies. Just see if you're not," she added maliciously.

"Come on Kelly, we're leaving," said Jess, dragging the distraught girl to her feet and leading her out of the hall and into the yard. Sophie followed them.

The dinner ladies were too stunned to stop them, but not speechless. They huddled together, Mrs Sour's leg having made a miraculous recovery, and vigorously pointed at the departing girls.

"Well I never," exclaimed Mrs Dumpling, her face puce with rage.

"How dare they ignore what we say," continued Mrs Salad, disgusted. "They should all be expelled."

"What we say is the only thing that matters at dinner time. We are the bosses," they chorused, so loudly that the rest of the children in the dining hall stopped eating. Several younger ones burst into tears thinking they had broken one minor rule or another. This pleased the dinner ladies.

"Keep quiet and eat your dinners," bawled Mrs Dumpling with evident satisfaction. A vestige of their authority had been restored.

During this outpouring of malice, Richard and Andrew finished eating their lunches and then joined the girls in the yard determined to shift the focus of the conversation away from the accusations of the dinner ladies and discuss the exciting lesson they had experienced in the dells and the possibilities it had revealed. They found the girls sitting on a bench in the yard overlooking the dells. They were transfixed by the strange plume of smoke which seemed to be beckoning them, accompanied by a curious light which illuminated it, coming from the depths of the park.

"It must be smoke from a fire," suggested Sophie, unhelpfully.

"It could be from a fire under a witch's cauldron," laughed Kelly.

Andrew wasn't so sure it was a laughing matter. "Interesting," he said. "I wonder if it could be something to do with the one Ms Salmon referred to."

The sighting served to heighten their desire to investigate the phenomenon, to see if it was real, or imagined.

"I think we should definitely pay the dells a visit," he said.

The others looked at each other, smiled and nodded.

"Definitely!" they all said.

"When?" asked Kelly.

"Tonight, of course," he replied.

"What time?" asked Sophie, beginning to wonder whether this was a good idea.

"Midnight!" exclaimed Jess, her face reflecting the excitement she was feeling. She loved a challenge. Richard was equally excited and nodded enthusiastically.

"Midnight, but that's the witching hour," observed Andrew, a little apprehensively. He was eager to return to the dells to find an explanation for the smoke and prove the rumours that were attached to it to be a story not based on fact, but to be the product of someone's overactive imagination. But at midnight, he was not so sure.

"Exactly," she said. "What better time? We'll be able to not only find the cause of the smoke, dismiss the rumours as pure fiction, and write the best story ever!"

Excited by Jess' speech they locked arms and whispered together.

"Midnight tonight!" they said and then ran to the other groups of children who were playing football, skipping, chase and other assorted games and joined in with the normal lunchtime activities, though their thoughts were firmly focused on the coming night's adventure.

Unknown to the 'sleuths' Mrs Turnip, a colleague and close friend of the other disgruntled dinner ladies, had overheard parts of their conversation. An evil smile, which did little to improve her craggy features, creased her face and she scuttled off to tell her friends about what she had heard, ignoring several crying, bleeding children who had accidentally fallen over and injured themselves. She had more important things on her mind than whingeing children, as she formed the beginnings of a plan for revenge on the horrible group of brats who could do no wrong. Her friends would like her idea and no doubt embellish it with some of their own nasty ideas!

As the four dinner ladies were leaving the school, having completed their lunchtime duties with more petulance than usual, thanks to Ms Salmon spoiling their fun when they were attempting to discipline the particularly ill-mannered group of brats who called themselves the 'Super Sleuths', their natural curiosity compelled them to look into her classroom as they passed by in the hope of being able to criticise the work she had been putting up on her walls that dinner time. They were astonished to see what she and her assistant had achieved. They were intrigued by the objects and characters on the wall frieze. It gave them further food for thought for the activities they were planning to put into place in the dells later that night. All they needed to complete their preparations was a simple phone call to an interested party who would add her own particular brand of wickedness to the forthcoming proceedings, of that they were certain.

Chapter 2

During the afternoon following their disappointing dinner time when their normal, uncaring behaviour had been disrupted by the interfering of Ms Salmon, Mrs Sour, Mrs Salad, Mrs Onion and Mrs Dumpling had gathered together at the latter's house to discuss their forthcoming activities for Halloween, an occasion they always celebrated in their own unique and bizarre way. This invariably involved dressing as witches, garbed in long black cloaks, partial face masks and mountains of make-up to complete their transformation for the evening's festivities. Once suitably attired, they engaged in traditional witch-like activities: dancing round a cauldron, pretending to fly on a broomstick, mixing potions which, together with some magic mumbo jumbo, would enable them to cast spells. These activities, usually oiled by the consumption of their favourite tipple, gin, took place in Mrs Dumpling's cousin's custom-built witches' lair, hidden in the second – or as they were often known because of their remoteness and inaccessible nature – secret, dells. Access to the den was possible through two passageways, both padlocked to prevent unwanted visitors. To further dissuade people from investigating their lair, and as a form of entertainment, one of their favourite activities in previous years had been to creep up on dog walkers exercising their pets on the nearby field at the top of the dells and leap out at them, then cackle raucously in their ears, threatening to transform them into pigs. But tonight was special, they'd keep all their nastiness for the so-called 'Super Sleuths'.

Having seen the detailed frieze created by the presumptuous Ms Salmon and irritated beyond belief by that group of odious children, the seed of an idea for revenge blossomed into a veritable banquet for the dinner ladies. Here they thought was an opportunity, not only to enjoy their usual Halloween celebration, but to enhance their pleasure by subjecting the vile brats to some terrifying experiences which they would remember forever, but not in a good way!

After their discussion, the dinner ladies spent the afternoon gathering together the equipment they needed to replicate the Halloween scene in the classroom. Some items, such as the cauldron, cobwebs and broomsticks, were already there, a leftover from last year's party. But this year was going to be different, very different. It was going to be a Halloween party with some special, if unwilling, guests, the horrible brats: Richard, Jess, Andrew, Sophie and Kelly. It was time for their comeuppance and with help from Mrs Dumpling's sinister cousin Gertie Grimbody and her scary, lugubrious friend, Ivan Killjoy, who hated the brats in question, as much, if not more, than she and her colleagues did, they would reduce the children to gibbering wrecks, which was no less than they deserved!

In order to set up the night's events, Mrs Dumpling contacted her cousin and they agreed to meet at the entrance of the secret passageway, a tunnel that was narrow and damp, and which led to the den.

The dinner ladies arrived at the agreed meeting place at the appointed time, but there was no sign of Gertie.

"Where is she?" grumbled Mrs Sour.

"Is she not coming to join the fun?" asked Mrs Onion.

"She'll be here, don't you worry," replied Mrs Dumpling. "She hates these horrible brats even more than we do. And don't ask why, it's a secret," she added, as she could see that the other ladies were eager to ask the question. "If you do it will only upset her, and you definitely don't want to do that."

The three dinner ladies gulped and nodded. They'd heard rumours about Gertie's venomous temper, which, when roused, resulted in violence against, and injury to, the offending parties.

Seconds later, they heard Gertie approach as she clumped heavily along the path to the secret door that led to the den, ripping branches off the bushes as she did so in order to create a path wide enough to enable her large, muscular body to pass through. On seeing Gertie's fearsome face and massive body, Mrs Onion, Mrs Salad and Mrs Sour immediately understood why Mrs Dumpling had suggested it would be a serious mistake to annoy her pugnacious cousin, and all three shivered uncomfortably.

Gertie glared at the intimidated dinner ladies with a look of utter contempt as she produced a skeleton key to open the door. After opening it, she led the way down to the den, munching a pork pie, with the nervous dinner ladies following her vast bulk at a safe distance.

Once inside, excitement was writ large on the faces of the women as they bustled around filling jars with ingredients, carving ghoulish faces on pumpkins, gathering logs for the fire and filling the cauldron with an unpleasant smelling liquid, showing an enthusiasm and energy completely absent in their roles as dinner ladies. Gertie spluttered instructions from her precarious position on a wooden stool positioned in the corner of the den next to a dangling, unpleasant looking effigy, whilst greedily tucking into her favourite snack, another voluminous pie.

Thirty minutes later, after consuming several scones as afters, Gertie nodded her approval of the dinner ladies' efforts to create an appropriate environment for the events to come.

Mrs Onion was more enthusiastic. "That's perfect. Just like the one in the brats' classroom," she said, proud of their collective efforts.

As preparations for their 'guests' were now complete the dinner ladies were in celebratory mood.

"When we 'persuade' the brats to join us we'll teach them a lesson they won't forget in a hurry," grinned Mrs Dumpling, looking at the cauldron and all the other Halloween items that adorned the den, with a rare sense of satisfaction.

"Learn 'em not to believe in witches," added Mrs Salad, smiling hideously.

"It'll do much more than that," interrupted Gertie, glaring at the dinner ladies with her demonic eyes boring into their heads. "I intend it to be their last, and very painful, lesson!"

"What do you mean?" asked Mrs Dumpling, nervously, fingers twitching in discomfort.

"I mean," snapped Gertie, "we, all of us, intend for this lesson to be their last as human beings! Don't we?"

The dinner ladies gasped in disbelief. They had only intended to terrify the children, frighten them out of their tiny, unpleasant minds, but what Gertie was suggesting sounded unacceptably horrendous, even to *their* malicious ears and they began to shuffle nervously away from her.

Realising that the dinner ladies' commitment to the painful removal of the brats from the face of the earth was not part of their plans for revenge, but very definitely essential to hers and Ivan's, she darted forward, grabbed hold of Mrs Onion and Mrs Salad and manhandled them towards Mrs Dumpling and Mrs Sour. She then fixed the quivering quartet with her demonic gaze, red eyes flickering ominously. The women were mesmerised by the movement; hypnotised, and immediately receptive to her evil suggestions.

Gertie smiled unpleasantly as she informed them of her wicked plan and the part they would play in it. Satisfied they understood their roles and would perform them without question, Gertie flicked her fingers and the dinner ladies returned to the here and now, looking slightly bemused, not understanding what had happened to them.

"Excellent, ladies; preparations are now complete. I look forward to receiving your message tonight informing me that the delinquents are ready, and of course unwilling, to sample the delights we have in store for them," she announced.

The dinner ladies smiled and nodded; they were excited by the thought of getting their own back on the vile 'Super Sleuths', though they had no idea of the nature of the punishment that Gertie and Ivan had planned for the children, or their part in it. Had they been aware of its criminal nature they would have stayed at home with their feet up watching the television and not venturing into the dells on what would prove to be a very fateful night. But, as they had no conscious idea of Gertie and Ivan's intentions, they were willing participants in what they imagined was going to be an entertaining night for them and an unpleasant one for the brats. They were right in one sense, but very wrong in another. This Halloween was going to play out very differently for all involved!

Now that the den had been set up to everyone's satisfaction and the dinner ladies had been tricked into playing a crucial role in her nefarious plan, Gertie returned to Cloggham Hall with a growing hunger, not only for food, but more importantly, revenge. *Past wrongs need to be put right and will be,* she thought happily, as she stomped up the passageway towards the exit leading to the Hall.

Relieved that Gertie had gone, the dinner ladies then decided on their own plan of action to determine who would do what, when and where, to be fine-tuned by information to be gathered later by listening to the conversation of the children after school.

Before they left the den in a state of euphoria, they decided to give themselves suitable witches' names. Mrs Dumpling was to be called Grizelda; Mrs Sour was to be known as Gizelda; Mrs Salad was Greta and Mrs Onion was to be called Grimelda. It was also agreed that Mrs Dumpling would bring along her three mischievous sons to help carry out their plan. They were to be dressed as goblins and were to be called Salvador, Leonardo and Raphael; they had aspirations to be artists—con artists!

As they left the passageway they noticed a curious mist drifting along the lower slopes of the dells.

"That's odd," observed Mrs Salad, pointing at the fog.

"It's autumn," said Mrs Dumpling. "It's often misty down there."

The others nodded sagely; Mrs Dumpling was always right. But what they didn't see was a mysterious plume of smoke which billowed out from somewhere in the depths of the wood behind them.

Chapter 3

The bell rang to signify the end of dinner time and herald the start of afternoon lessons. On entering the classroom Ms Salmon was pleasantly surprised to see Jess, Andrew, Richard, Sophie and Kelly already busily engaged in writing the introductions to their stories.

As the children had entered the classroom after lunch they had been astonished by the sight that greeted them. Ms Salmon and her wonderful assistant had transformed the classroom into a mini replica of the dells. They had created a spooky, exciting scene that mirrored their morning's experience in the dells, both real and imagined. Paper cobwebs dangled from the ceiling; a forest of cardboard trees had appeared over the sink area, surrounding the entrance to a cave. Situated in the centre of the opening was a black cauldron, covered in mystical symbols. Also in the cave were three hideous witches, dressed in flowing black cloaks, their long skeletal fingers protruding from frayed sleeves, long pointed noses inhaling the fumes from the pot. Behind them, lining the shelves, were jars of ingredients containing such delicacies as toads' legs, bats' wings, bulls' eyes and newts' tails, all ingredients for their vile concoction. Three broomsticks rested in the corner of the cave and a black cat lounged on a mat next to the fire. Behind the trees lurked two weird-looking creatures. They sported sharp noses, shiny green skin and long pointed ears that were parallel to the floor; sharp teeth protruded from their thin, mean lips; an unpleasant grin seemed to greet anyone who looked at them. There was also a pumpkin carved into the shape of a face on each of the children's tables.

The class were enthralled, slightly scared but, as Ms Salmon had intended, stimulated to write a story so exciting, possibly frightening, that both the writer and the reader would be drawn into it and want to read on. They all dashed to their desks. Once more they looked at the stimulating environment that their teacher had created, organised their notes from the morning's activities, looked at the success criteria and were writing before Ms Salmon could speak.

"I'm definitely going to have evil witches in my story," whispered Sophie, prophetically.

"Gruesome goblins are going to attack the main characters in mine," said Kelly.

"I've got a cauldron in mine and I'm going put you in it," laughed Scott.

Kelly was not amused and was about to administer some rough justice on her least favourite boy when Ms Salmon turned her attention from writing on the white board and faced the class. Instead of trying to hit her tormentor with her raised hand, she asked her teacher if she could borrow a rubber to erase a mistake. She gave him a look that would have turned most people to stone, but not

Scott, who didn't understand rejection.

"Yes of course, Kelly," she said, walking over to her to give her a rubber and also to see what the children were actually writing. She was surprised to read the same intriguing phrase beginning each story. *A mysterious plume of smoke rose from the skeletal trees.*

How interesting, she thought. *I'm looking forward to reading these stories already, even though they haven't been written!*

Recognising their enthusiasm for creating a story they would always remember, she said nothing and let them write, stopping them only occasionally so that an excited pupil could read out a section of their work which they were particularly proud of and which the rest of the class would be interested in.

To the Super Sleuths, the mysterious plume of smoke was more, much more, than the opening to a story, it was the beginning of an adventure that would begin at midnight. Had they known how fiction and reality were to become blurred by a series of bizarre and terrifying events their quest would have ended before it began. It would have been restricted to a paper exercise, but of course they didn't know that. Not yet!

Chapter 4

The bell tolled for the end of the school day and heralded the beginnings of an investigation into not only the source of the plume of smoke, which seemed to have sinister undertones, but also, if Ms Salmon was to be believed, to see if the long-standing rumours about the presence of a secret pagan society, engaged in diabolical rituals, deep within the undisturbed and thickly wooded part of the dell, where no one ventured at night, existed.

As soon as they were released from class, the intrepid Super Sleuths grabbed their coats, dashed out of the double classroom doors and sat on two of the benches that were positioned underneath a large, leafless, hornbeam tree. There they began to discuss in detail what, when and how they were going to investigate the unexplained happenings in the dells that they had heard about and in a sense had witnessed. Smoke didn't just appear from thin air. There may have been a simple explanation, but somehow it felt wrong to the group, and they trusted their collective instincts.

"We're all agreed then. We investigate tonight," said Richard, looking at the smiling, if slightly nervous, faces of his friends and fellow adventurers.

"What time should we meet?" asked Andrew, clearly

excited and wondering what equipment he needed to take with him in case of disaster.

"I can't wait," announced Jess, rubbing her hands together, eager to begin their latest adventure. "What about you two?" she asked, looking at Sophie and Kelly, whom she considered the weak links of their group.

Despite harbouring reservations about the wisdom of entering the dells in the dead of night to investigate a mysterious plume of smoke, a strange beam of light and the rumours of evil spells being cast on this one special night, they nodded their agreement, too frightened of Jess to do otherwise.

"What time shall we meet then?" asked Sophie nervously.

"Why, eleven thirty, of course. That will give us plenty of time to get deep into the secret part of the dells before the witching hour," Andrew beamed, checking his watch. "In eight hours' time, and the clock's ticking."

"Er, why then and not a bit earlier?" mumbled Kelly, confused and even less enthusiastic about this adventure than Sophie.

"Because midnight is the witching hour," explained Jess. "That's when we're most likely to find out what's happening."

"But why are we going?" whined Sophie, not liking the thought of this investigation. It was sounding more dangerous by the minute.

Jess was exasperated. "We're going to find out if the rumours are true that there are wicked people lurking in for midnight!

Scott followed them at a distance with a distinct spring in his step. He now knew where his classmates were heading and when, and nothing was going to prevent him from joining them, though he was soon to wish something had!

the dells."

"And if they are, do something about it," added Richard.

"But what if there are real witches there?" asked Sophie.

"I'm pretty sure there won't be. I think Ms Salmon told us a tall story in order to fire our imaginations for the purposes of writing an even more exciting story," he added, hoping that was the case, but was less confident than he sounded.

He then reached up to an overhanging branch of the hornbeam and quickly did ten pull-ups to ignite his muscles, sharpen his mind and diminish his doubts. Impressed more by Richard's deeds than his words, Kelly tried to do the same, but her fingers slipped off the branch she was trying to grip, and she collapsed in an untidy heap on the muddy ground just as Scott appeared. He again enjoyed a moment of Kelly's discomfort. He smirked at her misfortune, reached up to the same branch as the one Kelly had left earlier than she would have liked and attempted to show her how to do a successful pull-up, but promptly fell to the ground next to Kelly with an impressive splat. The others ignored both failed acrobats, who were glaring at each other, and continued to discuss the night's arrangements.

"It's settled then, we meet at eleven thirty," said Richard.

"At the corner of Ash Avenue," Andrew suggested. "It's near to where we all live and close to the school grounds."

"Can't wait," enthused Jess, dragging a soggy and still complaining Kelly to her feet.

"But it's very late," protested Sophie, beginning to regret her involvement with the group. "I might not be able to sneak out of my house. My parents stay up very late," she added, hoping that would be a good excuse for not going with them.

"Don't come then," snarled Jess. "Stay at home and sleep."

Sophie looked sheepishly at the others, including Kelly, who looked forward to the adventure. She couldn't back out and she didn't really want to, but the dells would be dark and probably dangerous. Then she remembered that Jess, Richard and Andrew would be there, and they were clever and strong; they would protect her if there was trouble. Also, she couldn't abandon her best friend Kelly, could she? Her thoughts were interrupted by a soggy Scott who had slowly regained his feet and his senses.

"If she doesn't want to go can I come instead?"

The others looked at each other askance. They knew what Scott was capable of, and it wasn't much!

"No he's not going instead of me," shouted Sophie, slightly hysterical. "I was only teasing you; of course I want to go with you."

A concerned Kelly asked, "But will you be able to get out of your house?"

"Yes, yes definitely!" she blurted, now desperate to visit the dells.

Deeply disappointed, Scott turned dis[c] away and pretended to leave them to [ ] preparations, but he didn't go far. He hid behin[d] trunk of the hornbeam tree and listened [ ] conversation. He was determined to go with the[m] or another.

A few metres away, four women were col[ ] children they reluctantly child minded, [ ] focusing on their needs by thrusting sweets [d] throats, even though the choking sounds comin[g] children's mouths suggested otherwise. Ho[w] women's attention was really elsewhere. They [ ] listening to the muffled complaints of their ch[ ] were instead straining their ears desperately [ ] eavesdrop on the conversation of the Super Sleu[ ]

"So that's it then. We meet on the corne[ ] Avenue at eleven thirty," Richard repeated so th[ ] would be late. They all nodded enthusiastica[ ] Sophie.

"What equipment should we bring with u[s] asked sensibly.

"Good question," said Andrew. "A torch [ ] useful. Phones are a waste of time: no signal, the[ ] a dead zone." A phrase that would come back to h[ ] and the rest of the group.

The four women, who were listening intently [ ] smiled at one another, shouted at their chil[ ] pretending to vomit and dragged them up the dri[ ] school gate where they finalised their own wick[ ]

Chapter 5

After going through the motions of minding the children in their care after school, and returning them to their parents, howling, as they'd been denied access to their phones, tablets, computers and televisions, the dinner ladies excused themselves from their other domestic commitments and assembled in the dells outside the padlocked gate that blocked the entrance to the witches' lair. Mrs Dumpling unlocked the gate with her own skeleton key and the four women entered the den in a frenzy of excitement. Once they'd lit the numerous lanterns that were strategically placed on the walls and hanging from the ceiling beams, they climbed into their waiting witches' outfits. They then carefully fixed their elaborate masks, slapped on make-up and completed their hideous appearance by donning a variety of greasy, green and black wigs.

They gazed in awe at each other.

"Oh how grotesque you look!" shrieked Grizelda, on gazing at Grimelda's appearance.

"You too look particularly hideous," she replied with a smile that threatened to crack her mask.

Greta was also impressed by Grizelda's appearance, but in a different way.

"You look positively beautiful, my dear."

"A pity I can't say the same for you, you monstrosity," she laughed, and all the dinner ladies, now transformed into witches joined in, cackling so loudly that the noise disturbed the sleeping bats that were dangling from the eves of the crudely thatched roof of the den. Angry at being disturbed, they swooped on the witches who grabbed their broomsticks and swatted them away.

Having persuaded the bats to relocate and find fresh victims, the witches returned to their main task which was to light the fire under the cauldron so that it would be bubbling nicely by the time the children were 'invited' to join the celebration, not knowing, of course, that they were going to be on the receiving end of a series of very unpleasant events that the witches had devised for them, with a little extra nastiness thrown in by Gertie.

"The brats are going to wish they'd never been born," squawked Grizelda, vigorously stoking the fire that Greta had lit moments before. The others giggled dementedly, and nodded their agreement.

Gizelda then began to pour some ingredients into the pot whilst Grizelda stirred the vile concoction with a giant spoon. Despite the clouds of steam from the 'broth', and smoke from the fire, excitement surged through the four of them and they burst into song. *Hubble bubble toil and trouble, leg of toad, eye of bull, fill my stomach till it's full*, and finished it with an ear-splitting cackle.

Satisfied that everything was ready, they waited patiently for the time immediately before the witching hour when each witch would enter the dells along a pre-planned route, knowing exactly where they were going and what they were going to do. Their plan was perfect; it couldn't fail.

"Revenge will be so sweet," said Grizelda, not seeing the squirrel that had observed the witches' antics, nor the conker that bounced off the back of her head, knocking her off balance. She crashed into Greta who narrowly avoided becoming an additional ingredient in the 'broth'.

"What was that?" she screamed seeing nothing out of the ordinary. The others looked, but could see nothing beyond their monstrous noses.

"You don't think that's an omen do you?" voiced Grimelda, suddenly unsure.

Grizelda dismissed the idea with a wave of her hand. "Probably a greedy squirrel carrying too many conkers, and dropped one," she laughed, but not for long as another conker hit her straight between the eyes, momentarily stunning her.

Enraged Grizelda screamed at the place where she thought the conker had come from and then threw a broomstick in the same direction. But the squirrels had long gone, leaping acrobatically from branch to branch back to their preferred vantage point where they could observe events unfold.

"It's a coincidence," Grizelda announced, hurriedly. "Nothing more," she added, trying to calm the nerves of her fellow witches who were beginning to wonder if they were not the only ones capable of creating mischief on this night of nights.

Their thoughts were interrupted by the appearance of Grizelda's sons.

"After you've changed into your goblin outfits," she bawled, "take these planks." She pointed to four lying on the floor. "And construct a bridge over the valley where it's narrow, but steep."

They nodded, picked up the planks and left the den through the tunnel which led to the stream, to build the bridge which would enable the witches to access the main pathway through the dells without having to use the log bridge, or go the long way round. They grinned; they were looking forward to this night, it was going to be a lot of fun for them, or so they thought.

"Right, we're ready. Let the show begin," snarled Grizelda.

The squirrels left their concealed observation post and bounded off determined to contribute to the night's events.

"The clock's ticking, ladies," announced Grimelda. "Are we all ready?"

"We're ready!" they cackled and grabbed their 'magic wands' and gazed into the bubbling contents of the cauldron as though it could foretell the future. If only they'd known!

Chapter 6

Richard and Andrew met each other on an unlit part of the street where they both lived; they didn't want to attract the attention of any concerned neighbours who may have intervened and returned them to their parents. It was, after all, eleven thirty on the 31st of October.

"No problem getting out without being noticed?" asked Richard.

"No, none at all. My parents are in a dead sleep," replied Andrew, grinning.

"I hope not!" exclaimed Richard, seeing the joke. "I had no problems either."

Just at that moment, Jess and Kelly appeared, waving enthusiastically.

"Hi guys," they shouted, clearly excited.

"Hi girls," the boys replied.

"All ready to go?" asked Richard.

"Can't wait to find out what's going on in the dells," replied Jess. "It can't be witchcraft; it doesn't exist."

At the mention of witches Kelly shrank into the shadows. She was here with the others, but she didn't really share their enthusiasm or belief. She'd read a terrifying book about what witches could do, and she was convinced they existed, but not, she hoped, in the dells. She was nervous, but determined to go with her friends.

"Right let's go then," said Richard, looking around to make sure they were alone. Satisfied that was the case, he was about to head off in the direction of the school when he stopped abruptly.

"Just a minute," he said, "we're missing a person."

"Sophie!" the others chorused.

"Has she decided not to come with us?" asked Andrew, looking at Kelly who shrugged her shoulders.

"I bet she's too scared," said Jess, who wasn't afraid of anything.

Kelly had been too worried about her own situation to have noticed her friend's absence.

"She told me she was definitely coming with us. I don't know why she's not here," answered Kelly, bemused.

"Maybe she couldn't sneak out," suggested Andrew.

"Let's run round to her house and see if we can help," said Richard, dashing towards the missing girl's home, which was in the next street. The others followed, with Andrew lagging behind as he was carrying a rucksack full of equipment. A minute later, having narrowly avoided several people stumbling out of the local pub, they arrived at Sophie's house and secreted themselves in her garden. Sophie's bedroom was on the first floor directly in front of them. The curtains were closed, and the room was shrouded in darkness.

"I bet she's forgotten and she's fast asleep," suggested Kelly.

Jess doubted this. "Well if she is I'll wake her up," she

said.

"How?" said Kelly. "You can't just knock on the door and ask if Sophie is coming out to play. Not at 11.31 p.m.!"

"I'm not going to do that, you halfwit. I've got something more subtle in mind."

Richard and Andrew looked at each other; Jess didn't usually do subtle. They watched aghast as she picked up a handful of soil and small stones from the garden border and threw them at Sophie's bedroom window. She scored a direct hit. The noise the impact made was surprisingly loud, but fortunately didn't shatter the glass as Richard and Andrew thought it might, knowing how strong Jess was.

"I didn't mean to throw it that hard," she muttered, fearing that she had cracked the window.

She needn't have worried for her plan worked perfectly as the glass stayed in one piece and Sophie's surprised face appeared through a gap in the curtains. She looked distressed. The others glanced at each other wondering what was wrong when a light was turned on in the hall. Then the front door of Sophie's house creaked open a fraction and a nose peeped out.

"Who's there?" shouted a nervous, but angry voice.

The children scrambled as quickly and quietly as they could behind a large rhododendron bush, hoping not to be seen or heard.

"Anybody there dear?" came a voice from somewhere deep within the house. It belonged to Sophie's mum.

"No I don't think so. I'll have a quick look outside."

The children huddled closer together in the

45

furthermost corner of the garden fearing that if Sophie's dad spotted them, their adventure would be over before it had begun. In the event, he took a couple of steps down the path, nervously looked around, saw nothing, shivered slightly and returned to the house.

"Nothing there. Must have been a pesky fox," he concluded, quietly closing the front door. The light was turned off in the hall, but one was switched on in the lounge, a room directly under Sophie's bedroom.

The group were dismayed. Sophie was stuck. Her parents were awake and vigilant. She threw her hands up in the air in despair and then opened her bedroom window. "I want to come with you, but I can't. As you can see my parents are still up and about," she sobbed, genuinely frustrated.

It looked as though Sophie's night was going to be a quiet one, unlike her friends when Andrew, having examined the front of the house in detail with his night-vision binoculars, came up with a solution.

"Look guys," he said pointing. "Look at that trellis with some sort of plant growing up it, probably a wisteria which has a root system that firmly attaches it to a wall."

The others looked closely at the front wall of the house and saw his point.

"I'll climb up and get her," volunteered Kelly leaping to her feet only to be restrained by Jess.

"I don't think so," she smiled.

"I'll go and see if it's safe," said Richard.

Before he did, Andrew quickly explained the plan to

Sophie who looked first at the trellis, then at the drainpipe that led up to it and finally at the height from her bedroom window to the ground. Her face immediately expressed doubt.

"It doesn't look very safe to me," she muttered, watching Richard adroitly climb up the drainpipe first and then onto the wooden framework holding the shrub, stopping when he was level with Sophie's bedroom window.

"Come on Sophie. It's quite safe; I'll help you."

Still not convinced but determined to give it a go, she eased herself out of her window, one leg at a time, gripping the surprisingly thick branches of the wisteria with her hands. She moved slowly, with Richard's help. Everything was going well until one of the cross members of the trellis snapped with a loud crack. As one of her hands was left holding a piece of wood that was no longer attached to the rest of the trellis she panicked, let out a small cry of anguish and swung dangerously away from the wall of the house, holding on grimly with her other hand. The watchers below gasped and covered their eyes. They couldn't bear to watch. Their friend was in danger and their adventure was going to be abandoned. It was, that is, until Richard caught Sophie's arm that was no longer responsible for her attachment to the wall and grabbed it to secure it to a piece of the trellis, which she clasped and clung to in desperation.

"You're okay now; just take your time. Spread your weight onto your feet and hands and you'll be fine."

Though not convinced, Sophie followed Richard's advice and after a few minor mishaps, she reached the safety of the ground. Her pale face reflected her discomfort, but that quickly faded as her friends greeted her warmly.

"Well done Sophie," said Kelly and Andrew.

Jess mumbled something under her breath and then said, "Let's go; we've only got twenty-seven minutes until the clock strikes midnight. The witching hour!" she added playfully.

Kelly and Sophie shivered. They didn't like the sound of witches. They didn't really like the sound of this adventure, but they were part of the group, and they didn't want to upset Jess. Nonetheless, Sophie thanked Richard for rescuing her. Then Jess set off running towards the school grounds. Only Sophie continued to have slight misgivings about the investigation, the others had extinguished all doubts and were excited by the prospect.

As they approached the school gate that led into the dells, a plume of luminous smoke appeared above the largely leafless horse chestnut and beech trees that dominated the dells.

"There it is again," said Andrew, pointing to the strange shape that the smoke had assumed. A mist swirled around their feet and covered the undergrowth, as a chill wind attacked their bones. A mysterious light flashed directly at them through the ever-increasing gloom, momentarily illuminating the smoke then it veered away transforming the trees' naked branches into skeletal fingers that swayed gently in the light breeze. They seemed to be beckoning the group into the depths of the dells. Kelly and Sophie were mesmerised by the light. Andrew was absorbed by the shape of the cloud of smoke that had by now totally obscured the thin sliver of the crescent moon.

"Twenty minutes to midnight. We need to find the source of the light and the plume of smoke and who's responsible for this strange phenomenon," said Andrew.

"I think it's the witches," said Sophie, clearly terrified by the thought.

"So do I," agreed Kelly.

"Let's go home," they said together, becoming more and more uncomfortable with the thought of this adventure.

Jess ignored them. She was obsessed with finding the cause by midnight, but she didn't know why.

"Please yourself. Come on boys," she said crawling under the padlocked metal gate.

Richard snapped Andrew out of his reverie and they both followed Jess. Kelly and Sophie were still staring at the light undecided as to what to do until Jess intervened hissing, "Come on or we'll leave you on your own!"

This had the desired effect, both girls suddenly aware that it was time to move, despite their reservations, which were increasing rather than diminishing by the second. They were convinced this adventure wasn't a good idea, and for once they were right! Sophie slithered under the gate, covering herself in mud. Kelly hated getting dirty. She knew of another, a better, way of getting into the dells. There was a gap in the metal railings where someone had forced them apart. It was just big enough for her small frame, or so she thought. One arm went through without a problem. Similarly, a leg. Then her head, but not her body. She was firmly stuck. The others hadn't noticed as they were too intent on moving carefully through the large clumps of grass and the sharp spines of the many bramble bushes to be aware of her absence. Suddenly the moon vanished; it was dark, very dark. The dense mist swirled and eddied over the prominent tufts of grass. The children had lost their bearings even though they knew the location of every blade. This was one of the areas that they had passed through earlier with their teacher and often provided an exciting environment for their normal adventure games, such as survival.

"I can't see where I'm going, even with my binoculars," whispered Andrew. "This is dangerous. There's a pond here somewhere. I'm going to risk turning my torch on for a second."

"No!" hissed Jess, knocking the torch out of his hand.

It landed with a splash in the pool of water he had been looking for.

"Oops, sorry," apologised Jess, regretting her action.

The impact of the torch hitting the water awakened the sleeping frogs who immediately burst into a croaky chorus of discontent. The children were stunned by the intensity of the awful din, but worse was to follow as the amphibians began to spit water at them with unerring accuracy, covering the faces of all four in a filthy, stinking slime.

"Normal frogs don't do that," observed Andrew,

wiping his face on his coat sleeve.

"These obviously do," said Richard, "but they shouldn't be able to. Something is weird here."

"And we are going to find out what?" snapped Jess, also wiping the slime off her face with her jacket sleeve.

"Perhaps we should go back home," suggested Sophie. "I don't think it's very safe here. What do you think, Kelly?"

The other three could guess what Kelly's answer would be when Sophie, having turned round to speak to Kelly said, "Where is she? She's not here."

Shocked, the others looked around and not wanting to alert anyone, or anything, that might be lurking, whispered her name. But, no Kelly, no reply! The silence was broken by a whimpering sound that floated through the mist and reached the bemused ears of Andrew.

"Wait! I can hear her. She sounds to be still at the gate and in some sort of trouble if I'm not mistaken."

"Stay here. I'll go back and see what the problem is," said Jess, thinking correctly that Kelly had taken the wrong option, again!

The rest crouched down hidden by the long, damp grass, cloaked in the cloying mist which clung to their clothes, rendering vision beyond thirty centimetres impossible. Jess carefully retraced her steps along the faint footprints that led from the gate and followed Kelly's moans. She encountered a series of minor mishaps, slipping in the mud and tripping over the rampant brambles that covered much of this part of the field immediately before the dells. Seconds later her face collided with the metal gate and Kelly's right arm. Ignoring the pain in her jaw she saw the problem immediately.

"Help me, please," whined Kelly. "I'm stuck."

Jess thought she deserved to be because of her stupidity, but didn't say so.

"Keep still," she ordered and pushed Kelly backwards with such force that she was catapulted out of her entanglement with the railings, landing in the muddy churned up area before the gate with a splat.

Jess suppressed a giggle, but said, "Stop playing with the mud; we've got a mystery to solve."

Soaked and muddy a miserable Kelly crawled under the gate, joining a grinning Jess on the other side. She was about to speak when Jess interrupted her.

"Hold onto my coat so you don't get lost and hopefully we'll find the others. If they're still alive," she teased.

Kelly wasn't impressed. Wet, cold and distressed, she wanted to go home to her nice, warm bed, but was too afraid of Jess to say so.

"Where are you, Richard?" whispered Jess, the seconds ticking by as doubts about the direction she was taking began to consume her thoughts; she could see nothing but darkness and the dense mist. No voice announced a nearby presence. She moved on slowly, more and more concerned, dragging a reluctant Kelly with her. She could feel her friend's tension increase as her grip on her coat tightened. Tentatively, she advanced forward a few more steps, stumbled over a large clump of grass and performed a forward roll down a short, but steep, slope.

She knew where she was heading: the pond, but couldn't stop herself sliding head first down towards it, closely followed by a reluctant Kelly whose knees were indelicately placed in her lower back. She braced herself for the inevitable impact of the freezing water and, in all probability, what would prove to be a soggy, and early, end to their adventure. She and Kelly wouldn't be able to continue even if they managed to extricate themselves from the foul, deep and smelly pond. Just as Jess' head was about to enter the water a strong pair of hands grabbed her flailing arms and yanked her away from her seemingly inevitable immersion. Confused, Jess looked up fearing the worst, but was greeted by Richard's beaming face.

"I know you're interested in zoology Jess, but I didn't think you'd want to study the frogs in their favourite habitat!"

Dragging herself to her feet Jess also managed a smile, thanking Richard.

"No I didn't fancy a practical lesson!" Then she remembered Kelly. "Where's...?"

"Relax Jess," soothed Andrew. "Me and Sophie rescued her."

A few seconds later when calm was restored, Andrew asked, "Are we all good to go. It's 11.42 p.m. Time's running out."

And so it was, but not in a way he could possibly have imagined.

Chapter 7

Richard led the way, carefully avoiding the many pitfalls that littered their path, which was almost totally obscured by darkness. The first obstacle they encountered was a fast flowing, but small stream that formed the boundary of the first dell.

A bridge into the unknown, thought Richard, as doubts about the investigation seeped into his brain. Beyond lay a wasteland of neglect: vegetation allowed to run wild, paths overgrown, wild animals rampant. Despite knowing this, all the children were excited, but some were also frightened. Kelly wanted to go home. Sophie wished she'd stayed in bed. Andrew was consulting his watch; time was running out if they were to find the source of the mysterious plume of smoke by midnight, the witching hour.

They reached the stream in single file. Richard leapt across and landed safely, as did Jess. Andrew stumbled slightly but still made it to the other side without injuring himself. Sophie hesitated. She didn't really want to cross because if she did it meant she was committed to the adventure, but was persuaded to do so by Jess. Kelly was last. She could see only vague, shadowy figures waiting for her on the other side. She looked behind her; should she go back? Then she thought she saw a movement in the mist, heading her way. A cold chill ran down her spine and she jumped over the stream like a gazelle, easily landing on the other side.

"Well done. That was a leap of faith and took some courage," whispered Richard, knowing Kelly would prefer not to be involved in the adventure.

"I knew you could do it," said Sophie, smiling.

Kelly was still staring blankly behind her.

"I thought I saw someone, or something, in the mist, moving towards me. That's why I jumped so far," she explained.

Concerned, the others peered into the gloom, but saw nothing, only swirling mist.

"Perhaps it was a tree that moved in the breeze," suggested Andrew, his pocket binoculars proving useless in the darkness.

"Or it might be a witch," cried Sophie, fearing the worst. "Coming to get us," she added edging closer to Jess, who was concerned, but didn't show it.

Unable to offer an explanation, Richard decided to move off into the dells. Almost immediately they encountered difficulties. Not being able to see beyond their noses they stumbled into thick brambles that clawed at their clothes, scratching their legs and hands, and were stung by clumps of stinging nettles.

"Ouch that hurt," cried Sophie, as a thorn attached itself to her left hand.

"Quiet," hissed Jess. "We don't want to advertise the fact that we're here."

Sophie nodded and kept the agony to herself. As they moved deeper into the dells the bushes and undergrowth became thicker and more impenetrable. Progress was slow and painful.

An owl suddenly hooted and split the eerie silence; everyone froze and then instinctively ducked as they heard the flapping of large wings as the raptor burst out of the darkness and swooped down on them, outstretched talons heading directly for Sophie's crouching body. Jess spotted the danger and reacted instantly by diving onto her uncomprehending friend, her momentum plunging both of them into a compact bush. The owl vanished as quickly as it had appeared.

As Richard and Andrew helped the two dishevelled girls back onto their feet by, twigs and leaves sticking to their clothes and their hair, a stunned Kelly said, "What was that? I thought owls only ate mice and other rodents, not children."

"Yes, usually only small animals," confirmed Andrew, gasping for breath after his exertions. "But nothing seems to be normal tonight."

"You mean witchcraft was responsible for the attack?" mumbled Kelly, afraid to say it aloud.

"Nonsense," said Jess. "It simply mistook Sophie for a large rat!"

The boys smiled; Kelly sniggered, but Sophie scowled; she didn't like being called a rat.

Shifting the focus back to their quest to discover the source of the smoke Andrew said, "We need to find the path we used during the lesson."

"I agree, but that's easier said than done in the pitch black," said Richard.

The others said nothing but nodded their agreement. Richard moved on, his hands dripping blood from his battle with the brambles. The rest followed in single file, tension rising as they feared another attack of some kind, unsure whether it would be from a natural source or, worse, a supernatural one. Kelly and Sophie were at the back jostling for position; neither wanted to be last, traditionally the most vulnerable and dangerous place to be.

The ubiquitous gloom felt as though it was gluing Richard's eyelids together; the others were also experiencing a feeling of helplessness as they were lost, paradoxically, in a place they knew like the back of their hands. The ominous darkness felt to be pressing down on them as they stumbled and slipped along the uneven, narrow and indistinct pathway they were trying to negotiate. They knew where they were heading, towards the second dells which were no more than a few hundred metres away, but in the dense mist, it seemed like kilometres as their progress was so slow and laboured. However, urgency was at the forefront of their thinking, they needed to locate the source of the plume of smoke before the clock struck twelve as they thought that was the time when something diabolical was going to happen.

"I really don't like this fog," voiced Andrew. "It's unnaturally thick and opaque."

"We've got to keep going," whispered Richard.

"We've got to find the source of the smoke, and quickly."

"Yes, time is running out," added Jess, bringing her watch closer to her eyes so she could read the dial.

"If we don't find it in time what's going to happen?" asked Sophie, alarmed.

"Are we going to die?" muttered Kelly, her legs turning to jelly at the thought.

Though they didn't think they were going to breathe their last any time soon Richard, Jess and Andrew shared an uncomfortable feeling about midnight and the disaster it might bring. Sensing Andrew and Jess' growing frustration at their inability to move swiftly towards their goal, and fear in Sophie and Kelly, Richard resolved to increase the speed of their movement, but despite his best efforts achieved only limited results. The faster they tried to move the more they skidded and slipped on the treacherous surface and blundered into the dying, but cloying, undergrowth, colliding with saplings, tree stumps and bushes.

"We're getting nowhere," said Richard, frustrated, sweat pouring from his brow.

"Unfortunately, I think you're right," said Andrew. "In fact, I think we're going in ever-decreasing circles!"

Their conversation was truncated by a cry for help from Kelly who had tripped over an exposed root and plunged into a thick bush.

"Where are you?" cried the distraught and temporarily entangled girl.

"Here!" rasped Jess turning just in time to observe

Kelly stagger drunkenly from her encounter with numerous branches, lose her footing and stumble into a bemused Andrew, just as a huge carved, orange orb landed with a splat on the spot where he had been standing before Kelly's timely intervention. On impact the pumpkin, surprisingly, remained intact; it's grotesque, carved facial features staring scarily at them. Startled, they all edged away from the monstrous fruit.

"Where did that thing come from?" shouted Jess, looking up for its likely starting point, but she could see only darkness and hear the faint rustle of leaves and branches being disturbed high above them.

"Big conker," grinned Kelly, a nervous twitch suggesting she was more worried than amused by the sinister object's inexplicable appearance.

"Stupid joke," chastised Jess, angrily, who didn't cope well with events beyond her understanding and control.

"Another mystery," observed Richard.

"How could that happen?" asked Andrew, baffled.

"Somebody must have placed it in the tree," suggested Richard.

"And I bet it wasn't a squirrel," added Sophie. "It's too big!"

The others, including Jess, smiled at their friend's attempt to lighten the mood. But they were increasingly alarmed by their situation. They knew they were not alone in the dells on this fateful night. Someone, or something, was not only watching them, but actively interfering with their progress. They didn't know who or why, but they were aware that they had to move on; time was ticking away!

But before they continued their expedition Andrew knelt down in the mud and examined the carved face on the pumpkin more carefully. "Look at its face," he said. "It's contorted in agony."

"Do you think it's another message?" squealed Sophie.

"If it is perhaps it's suggesting we should abandon our mission," he said, not sure whether to carry on or return home, unlike Jess, who knew exactly what they should do.

"This message, or whatever it is, just makes our investigation even more intriguing. We've got to find out what's going on; where the plume of smoke is coming from, what it means and who's responsible for it."

Inspired by Jess' words, Richard said, "I agree completely. We have to keep going." With that, he set off. "Keep close to me," he urged. "I think I know where we are." He didn't but he thought it would make the others feel more confident if he said he did.

As Richard led the way up the muddy slope as quickly as he could, ever conscious of the ticking clock, only Andrew and Jess could keep up with him. As the mist became even thicker, the silence deeper, the atmosphere more sinister, the other two fell behind, with Kelly at the back and she was losing contact with Sophie and beginning to panic.

"Wait for me Sophie," she wailed. But Sophie didn't hear her, she was too intent on catching up with the others who had paused to wait for their slower friends. But Kelly had lost contact with them and was lost.

"This way," hissed Jess, hearing Sophie approach, but she couldn't see her, nor could Sophie see Jess until she collided heavily with Andrew, knocking him into some bracken which softened his landing, but bruised his pride.

"Sorry," she mumbled, as Richard helped him out of the clinging vegetation.

"Where's Kelly?" hissed Jess, fearing the worst as she couldn't see her.

"Behind me," said Sophie, turning round expecting to see her friend who wasn't there! "I-I don't understand. She was a minute ago."

"Oh no, not again," said Jess, kicking a bush in frustration.

"Listen, I can hear something," said Andrew, as something flapped close to their heads. It was quickly followed by another and another.

"Bats," whispered Richard.

"Are they vampires?" asked Sophie gripped by fear. Before the others could answer, a bat landed on her neck and started to nibble her flesh. She was about to scream when Jess' hand closed over her mouth. Jess then swatted the hungry mammal away in one movement.

Before they could fully recover their senses, a faint glow in the near distance paralysed them.

"W-what's that?" stammered Andrew, pointing at the twin orange lights that partially illuminated the gloom which enveloped them.

Richard was transfixed, as was Jess. They both stood

still and stared at the menacing sight. Unfortunately, Sophie didn't and collided with Jess' elbow causing her to be catapulted backwards into an enormous cobweb from which she struggled to free herself, the spider's strong mesh enveloping most of her body.

Ignoring Sophie's discomfort, Jess whispered in Richard's ear, "What do you think it is?"

"I don't know, but it looks threatening to me," he replied, preparing himself for action.

Jess nodded and did the same. Andrew urged caution. A distressed Sophie still trying to extricate herself from the sticky strands of the web announced a little too loudly, "I think it's a monster! Let's run!"

Having freed herself, she was about to do so when Jess grabbed her arm and prevented her from moving, anywhere. "Quiet," she hissed, "it's not a monster, but it might be part of the explanation for the plume of smoke."

Richard was continuing to stare fixedly at the lights which appeared to be flickering. Were they getting closer, or was it his imagination? The brightness seemed more intense than it was seconds before.

Andrew confirmed his fears. "I think, whatever it is, is coming towards us," he muttered, backing away, only to be stopped by Jess, still clutching the wriggling Sophie who was continuing to attempt to dash off.

"Wait, don't move," she ordered, quietly, as she could see that Richard was clearly determined to prevent the person, or creature, from attacking them.

He knelt down poised for action. An owl hooted; it

seemed like a signal. A bat stirred from the trees and flapped close to the quartet's startled heads. Jess tensed her muscles: she too was ready to tackle whatever was threatening them. Richard intervened by stepping in front of her and moving forward as he had decided that he should be the one to confront the danger.

It's now or never, he thought and launched himself at the tall, stationary, shadowy figure, hitting it in the midriff with his powerful shoulders. As a result, both crashed into the undergrowth in a tangle of interlocking limbs. The others were mesmerised by the events and held their breath as Richard and the creature disappeared into the darkness, accompanied by a muffled crashing noise which sounded like two bodies, wrestling ferociously. The din was immediately followed by the appearance of the object containing the two blazing lights which at first swayed, seemingly suspended in the air, and then accelerated towards them. They crouched down, hands covering heads as the lights neared them, becoming brighter as they did so. Suddenly the ghastly orange orb was hovering directly above their heads then dropped vertically, and spectacularly, into Sophie's upturned arms. She gazed at it in horror realising that she was holding the monster's decapitated head! She couldn't tear her eyes away from it as flames flickered ominously beneath its translucent skin. Her eyes bulged in disbelief. Was it going to explode? She opened her mouth to launch a scream that would have woken the dead when one of Jess' hands filled the space between her parted lips and the other grabbed the 'head'.

"Don't even think about it!" she hissed. Sophie didn't; she couldn't because she had fainted.

Andrew grabbed the orange orb off Jess and examined it carefully and announced, "It's only another pumpkin with a spider inside crawling around a couple of candles! The spider must have hitched a ride on Sophie."

Jess smiled with relief, but not for long as Andrew continued his description. "Look at the pumpkin's face, its mouth is carved in the shape of a cruel grin. What could that mean?" he pondered.

Smile gone, Jess observed, "Another omen, but not a good one. In fact, probably just the opposite."

Just at that moment Richard reappeared holding a tatty jacket and a pair of ripped trousers, straw sticking out of the numerous holes that punctuated the clothing. Jess and Andrew moved towards him smiling broadly, delighted to see their friend was unhurt.

Richard didn't return the smile, he was frowning. "Look at this," he said.

"It's only a scarecrow," observed Andrew, relieved.

Jess was more cynical. "But how did it get here and why?" she quizzed, scratching her head in consternation whilst giving Sophie a gentle nudge with her foot in order to speed up her return to the land of the living.

"I think this proves that someone is trying very hard to frighten us off. They don't want us to discover the source of the plume of smoke," said Richard brushing the straw from his clothes and then throwing the remains of the scarecrow into the bushes, startling a watching squirrel into a hurried exit. "There must be some evil masterminds behind what's happening in the dells tonight and they're clearly determined to keep whatever is going on from our prying eyes."

"But no one knew we had decided to investigate the strange phenomenon," said Andrew, baffled.

The others shrugged their shoulders not understanding anything about what was happening. Had they known what was soon to befall them they wouldn't have accepted Jess' next statement so readily.

"Well, it's not working," she declared, as she was, like Richard and Andrew, more determined than ever to solve the mystery, unlike a now fully conscious Sophie who wanted to go home. She hated pumpkins, spiders, the dark and the dells.

Up in the trees the squirrels were carefully observing the children's actions, but they weren't the only ones watching, other interested parties were waiting to intervene, though the sleuths were unaware of this, or indeed, of the macabre events that were soon to transform the nature of their quest from an investigation into a horror show in which they were to play the part of the hapless victims.

"Follow me and keep close," said Richard as he moved carefully and slowly along the narrow, uneven path strewn with leaves and broken twigs, towards the secret dells where he thought the source of the smoke, and the mystery, might be. Andrew and Jess did so. A grim determination drove them on; they weren't going to be intimidated. Sophie reluctantly brought up the rear; every step was a nightmare for her. She just wanted it to end and go home as she was sure Kelly had already done. Her thoughts were interrupted by more bad news.

"There's something coming this way!" exclaimed Andrew, urgently. "Something large and on the ground, but it doesn't sound like Kelly."

Terror struck the group like a sledgehammer.

"Quick, down," Richard commanded, sensing the sound was created by hostile footsteps.

They all slumped to the ground, desperately trying to disappear under the rhododendron bushes and the piles of decaying leaves. They could see another light, different to the ones they had just encountered, shining dimly in the near distance, slowly heading in their direction. It was accompanied by a strange noise, the sound of voices, but not ordinary voices. They sounded distinctly croaky. As the children tried to bury themselves still deeper under the fallen leaves, they then recognised the sound, a hideous, high-pitched cackling sound that was getting louder, the light shining more brightly as the owners of both neared their hiding place.

I knew I should have stayed at home, Sophie thought. Jess was looking for a weapon. Andrew was thinking it was twelve minutes too early for witches to appear, if indeed they were witches. Richard was worried about their perilous position and the bizarre obstacles that had already been thrown in their path, but was more concerned about what had happened to Kelly, fearing the worst.

He needn't have worried. Kelly was safe, for now. Having lost contact with Sophie, she had angrily kicked out at a pile of leaves, which were not leaves, but a rat enjoying a quiet supper until Kelly's foot struck. It scampered off squealing in one direction whilst Kelly did the same in another. She lost her footing as she blundered through the dense vegetation, slipped and slid into the hollow of a large tree trunk where she bashed her head, shaking the tree and waking up the slumbering red squirrels in their drays high up in the branches, and knocked herself out cold.

Safe in her involuntary resting, place she was blissfully unaware of the cackling creatures that passed a couple of metres away from where she was slumped, just as they were oblivious to her presence. Had the witches known she was there they would have paused in their journey to deal with Kelly, but, as they knew nothing of her position, or predicament, they carried on gleefully. What fun they were going to have tonight. Everything had been arranged; it was all ready. All it needed was children, willing, though that was unlikely given what was in store for them, or unwilling. Though their heavy long black cloaks snagged on the bushes and trailed in the mud they made surprisingly good progress through the mist towards their intended destination deep in the murky depths of the secret dells. Whatever minor discomfort they were experiencing they knew it was nothing compared to what the vile children were going to suffer at their malicious hands. The clock was ticking, and the pot was boiling!

Chapter 8

As the sounds slowly ebbed away and the immediate danger seemingly gone, Richard expressed his fears about their missing friend and whispered, "Any sign of Kelly?"

The others looked around and could only just see themselves, but no one else. They were all stunned, despite the terrifying noise, the presence of whoever, or whatever was making it and the inexplicable appearance of the pumpkins, they expected to see Kelly's smiling face emerge from the darkness. When she didn't only Sophie reacted.

"I'm going back for her."

"No. Stop, it's too dangerous, we don't know what horror is lurking down there," said Jess.

Unusually, Sophie ignored Jess and stood up, took a step in the direction of the stream, and promptly slipped, and slid down the muddy slope. Richard made a vain but brave, attempt to stop her, diving to grab her leg, but missed. She quickly vanished out of sight down the hillside, careering through bushes, stopping only when she collided with the hollowed-out tree trunk in which Kelly's unconscious body was slumped.

Stunned, bruised and scratched, Sophie dragged herself to her feet, shook her head and then panicked. What had she done? She had left the relative safety of the group to look for Kelly, who could be anywhere in the thick fog, in the middle of the night—and not any night, but Halloween, the night according to local legend, and Ms Salmon, when wicked witches lurk in the dells and cast evil spells, particularly on innocent children like her and her friends. A tear seeped from her eye. She didn't know what to do; she'd no idea where the others were. She collapsed onto her knees, sobbing quietly.

"Don't cry my dear," murmured a voice, a kindly voice.

"I-I can't help it," she spluttered. "I've lost my friends. I'm stuck in this horrible wood, and I don't know where I am."

"You're safe with me little girl," wheedled the woman, as she took hold of Sophie's arm and gently helped her to her feet. "I'll look after you," she mumbled.

"Thank you," said Sophie, gazing up at the woman's face to see if she looked as kind as she sounded. She didn't. What Sophie saw, to her horror, was a hideous face bristling with warts, a large, crooked nose, one eye glowing an emerald green, the other a vivid red, lips curled into an evil sneer which revealed a solitary tooth protruding from the roof of her mouth. The apparition bent down and spat her foul breath into Sophie's face.

"Come with me little girl you'll be quite safe," she repeated, increasing her grip on Sophie's arm.

"I don't want to. I want to go home," sobbed Sophie, realising this woman was no ordinary woman, and possibly a… a… w—She couldn't even think it.

"I think I'll go home on my own. I remember the way now," said Sophie, trying to disentangle herself from the woman's vice-like grip and failing to do so.

"Oh I can't let you do that; it's not safe," snarled the woman, her eyes gleaming brighter as her grip on Sophie's arm tightened still further.

"Get off you're hurting me," she squealed, still trying to pull away, but only succeeding in making the pain worse.

The woman's face cracked into a grin. "This is just the beginning. Your worst nightmare is about to commence," she snorted putting her free hand in her pocket and pulling out a short, but heavy stick. "First of all, I'm going to scramble your feeble brain and then I'm going to turn you into a toad."

As she raised her hand to administer the blow, a shower of conkers rained down on her head and body. She dropped the wooden baton and released Sophie's arm as she looked up for the source of the barrage and tried to protect herself from the bombardment, cursing loudly and issuing dire threats to the unknown perpetrators.

Sensing an opportunity to escape, Sophie grabbed the stick, swung it wildly in the direction of the woman, connecting painfully with her left knee. The woman dropped to the floor clutching her leg.

"You vile child. You'll pay dearly for that when my friends arrive. Help! I'm being attacked by vicious thug," she began to shout, but was prevented from broadcasting her woes when a large conker entered her capacious, and open, mouth effectively preventing her from uttering another word.

Sophie had seen enough; it was time to go. She was about to blunder off into the darkness, hoping it would lead her out of the dells when a foot shot out of the hollow tree, tripped her up and sent her tumbling down another muddy slope, one that led to a fast-flowing stream. The offending foot belonged to Kelly who was just regaining consciousness.

"Oh no, what have I done? I'm sure that was Sophie," she mumbled as her friend quickly shot out of sight. She crawled out of the hollow, ignored the woman who was rolling around in the mud and leaves, clutching a leg with one hand and trying to extricate the conker from her mouth with the other. As Kelly stood up wondering in which direction Sophie had departed, a choice was made for her as a conker struck the top of her head, knocked her off balance and down the same slope as Sophie, and then ricocheted onto the end of the woman's snout, which erupted into a volcano of blood! Seconds later, Kelly's downward momentum was stopped a metre away from the rushing water by something solid: Sophie's head!

"Found you at last," she said, wiping the mud from Kelly's face with her sleeve and smiling for the first time. But then her countenance darkened. "Did you see that dreadful woman? She grabbed my arm; she was horrible, I think she was a wi…"

"A witch," said Kelly.

"Yes," replied Sophie, "I think she must have been.

She was going to cast a spell and turn me into a toad!"

Before Kelly could react, they heard the snap of a twig. They both froze. Was she coming to get them? Fear rippled down their spines. They couldn't hide, they couldn't move. They looked at each and then peered into the gloom, but could see nothing but darkness. Then a shadowy figure began to slowly emerge from the mist edging closer and closer to the terrified girls. They couldn't speak; their mouths wouldn't work. They were paralysed. The figure moved closer, the darkness parted, the girls held their breath. What sort of monster was going to attack them? And then Scott appeared in all his glory!

"Hi girls. I thought I'd join in on your little adventure," he announced, grinning broadly.

The girls collapsed onto the ground. For the first time in their lives they were pleased to see Scott, well almost.

"What's going on?" he asked, surprised, but pleased, by their reaction.

"Lots," said Kelly, still recovering from the shock of seeing Scott rather than some kind of monster.

"None of it good," added Sophie.

"But how did you know we were going to explore the dells tonight?" Kelly asked, still bemused by Scott's presence.

"Easy, I overheard the plans you were making in the yard and when you were on the bench outside our classroom. So, I sneaked out of my house and tried to follow you, but I lost you in the mist."

"He must have been the shadowy figure you saw,"

said Sophie.

"Probably," answered Kelly, "but the figure seemed more sinister somehow—"

Her explanation was cut short by a scream.

"Help me, I've been savaged by a monstrous thug!" croaked the woman, having successfully removed the blockage from her throat.

"I see what you mean about not being good," muttered Scott, badly shaken. It began to dawn on him that this wasn't going to be the fun adventure he thought it would be. For once he was correct.

Chapter 9

Higher up the slope, Richard, Andrew and Jess had heard muffled voices of anguish and rage coming from somewhere in the dells. The mist and darkness obscured the sound and made it difficult to determine the direction of the source.

"It sounded to be coming from somewhere in front of us," observed Jess, about to set off in that direction when Andrew interrupted.

"Wait," he said and removed his compass from around his neck. He peered at it in the hope that he would be able to work out which way they should head next after investigating the ominous sounds. Unfortunately, the compass was broken. "No help from the compass," he announced. "It must have smashed when I dived onto the floor."

"Let's just head towards where we think the noise came from," suggested Richard. "The girls might be there and it's also in the direction we need to go, if we're going to find the source of the mystery."

"I agree," said Jess. "If Sophie and Kelly are not there they've probably gone home and are back in their comfortable beds, snoring the night away."

Andrew and Richard smiled briefly, both thinking the

idyllic picture Jess painted was highly unlikely. They feared the girls were more probably in deep trouble.

The trio carefully edged out of their hiding place as quietly as the snapping twigs and rustling leaves would allow and continued their quest, guided by the narrow gap between the ubiquitous brambles and ferns that created a path, of sorts, deeper into the dells and closer to the solution to the mystery of the smoke and the ominous rumours that surrounded it. Despite slipping and sliding and tumbling into bushes, they made reasonable progress and reached the main pathway that ran through the middle of the dells. On reaching it, they stopped and listened carefully for the sounds of danger and looked for Sophie and Kelly. They heard only silence and saw nothing.

"No sign of them," said Richard.

"As I thought. They must have gone home," said Jess, failing to hide her disgust.

Richard still wasn't convinced that Jess' assessment of Sophie and Kelly's location was correct, but recognising where they were, from a large rock that was positioned at the side of the path, said, "We'll carry on without them. Let's go to the other side of the path and quickly head towards the log bridge which we have to cross."

"Yes, it's the best way to get to the secret dells, the darkest part of the park," agreed Jess.

"Which is where the smoke must be coming from," said Andrew, hesitantly, nerves beginning to affect his voice, his confidence waning badly. He wasn't as adventurous as the two, but he was brave, and he was determined to solve the mystery, even if it meant entering the second dells, the most densely wooded, unkempt part. The part with neglected gardens, abandoned to nature for years, untouched by human hand, but not, he feared, by those of the supernatural!

The route to the log was, like everywhere else in the dells, muddy, slippery and dangerous. The treacherous sloping ground was also obscured by dense vegetation consisting of ferns and giant, spiky rhubarb like plants whose spines were as sharp as needles. Slowly, carefully, Richard and Jess negotiated a way safely through the massive plants without incident. Andrew was less fortunate and fell behind the other two as his progress was halted by contact with the sharp spikes of one of the plants. He squealed as acute pain ripped through the hand that made contact with one of the needles.

"Wait," he cried, but the sound of his voice was muffled by the cloying mist and his voice was lost to the others who had already reached the log bridge. They knew what it looked like, it was narrow and solid, but they could only see a metre in front of them and they didn't like what they saw. The log was drenched in moisture and covered in slimy, green moss.

"Crossing that is going to be difficult and dangerous," said Jess, looking down underneath the makeshift bridge to the fast-flowing stream that she could hear, but not see, some five metres below.

"But it's our only way," said Richard, preparing himself for the challenge.

"I'll go first," said Jess, pushing past her startled friend, and beginning to crawl slowly and carefully along the treacherous log.

Richard watched her disappear into the gloom with bated breath.

"Be careful," he whispered, but she'd already vanished.

"I'll go next," said Richard, turning to Andrew, but he wasn't there!

"Andrew, Andrew! Where are you?" he hissed, distraught at the loss of another of his friends.

Worryingly, there was no reply. Richard was torn between following Jess across the bridge to confront whatever was waiting for them, or go back and see if Andrew was okay, not injured in any way. He decided to do neither and wait for Andrew. He was sure that Jess would make it across the log with little difficulty, despite the conditions; she'd done it many times in the past, though not when it was pitch-black and shrouded in mist. But she was skilful and resourceful; he was confident that she would be waiting for him on the other side.

The seconds ticked by; no sign of Andrew, although Richard could hear a muffled noise, which sounded like a voice, a voice in distress. But where was it coming from? The mist and echoes distorted the direction from which the sound emanated. It seemed to be bouncing off the trees all around him. This persuaded him to go back and look for Andrew who he was now convinced was in danger. He turned away from the log and scurried back up the muddy slope, clinging on to the bushes that populated his route back to the main path.

When he reached it moments later, mud dripping from his hands, he stopped unsure of where to go next. He listened for a sound, a clue, that would indicate Andrew's whereabouts. The only thing he could hear was his own heartbeat, racing through the exertion of climbing the steep slope, and the perilous nature of his situation. He was alone, his friends had gone missing in the hostile environment of the dells, it was dark and misty, he could hardly see beyond his nose and, incredibly, he was lost, time was ticking away, twelve o'clock was fast approaching. What horrors would midnight unleash on him and his friends, who were all, he was sure, feeling like he was, abandoned and alone? There was no sign of Andrew, so he slithered down the slope, back to the log.

Andrew had not only lost his friends, but he had lost his way, physically and mentally. He, too, had slipped down a slope, a different one, taking branches off trees with him as he desperately tried to slow his descent, but failed to do so, stopping only at the feet of a gruesome looking woman draped in black with a splurge of red on one sleeve. She had a long, crooked nose, a mouthful of black teeth and breath that could strip paint. Her crimson eyes bored into his brain.

"Let me help you up," she said, offering a gnarled and hairy hand.

He recoiled in horror, tried to stand up, slipped, banged his head on a rock and slowly sank into a puddle, out cold.

"One down, four to go," muttered the hag, poking Andrew with her walking stick to see if he was conscious. He wasn't. She put two fingers in her mouth and whistled a mournful tune, which attracted a vile-looking creature, a goblin, and a swarm of bats that rained down on the woman, who tried to fight them off with her stick, and on the unconscious Andrew, on whose neck they landed on and began to nibble. As the teeth of one bat sank into his neck, he regained consciousness. Instantly realising what was happening, he was being savaged by not only a bat, but a vampire bat, a bloodsucker that would turn him into a zombie! He could feel the bat's teeth sinking deeper into his flesh. He tried to tear it off, but he couldn't, his fingers were caked with slimy mud and slipped off the creature's foul body.

"Save me," he garbled. "I don't want to become a zombie!"

The old woman tottered closer to him, watching the bat savage his skin. Her eyes blazed with joy as the bat munched away. She was enjoying this moment, revenge was sweet. This was an aperitif; the main course was to follow, and it would be a banquet. She waved her stick in the air, as though it were a wand; sparks flew from the end of it and the bats vanished into the mist, screeching in frustration. They were replaced by the weird looking creature who hopped from one spindly leg to the other, clearly overjoyed with what he had just witnessed.

"Remove this worm," screeched the woman, pointing

at the bleeding and semi-conscious Andrew. "Take him to the special room, the hello and goodbye room!"

The powerful goblin did as he was bid. He grabbed Andrew's collar, pulled him to his feet and pushed him along the path, keeping him upright as he stumbled and tripped, his legs not yet working properly. The creature roughly guided the limp boy through the murky darkness to the entrance of a wide drainage channel which was illuminated by a dull green light that was shining from a lantern, partially concealed by a fern. Rough hands pushed Andrew head first into the metal cylinder, sending him floating across the surface of the shallow water that was flowing along the base of the large drainage pipe. Andrew was barely conscious; at first he thought he was flying, then drowning as the water intermittently washed over his head.

Was this what fate had in store for him, he thought, a watery end? It wasn't. The rough hands forced him to his feet and pushed him towards a low passageway, again containing flowing water. Andrew vaguely recognised it as the culvert that joined the first dells to the secret dells and was usually blocked by a padlocked, steel gate, but there was no sign of it now as he splashed and staggered through the confined space jostled by the creature until they reached the other side of the passageway. Immediately Andrew's nose was assaulted by the unmistakeable smell of burning wood, and his ears by the sound of something boiling. He could almost taste the stench of a foul broth cooking in a pot. His heart missed a beat. Could the fire be the source of the mysterious plume of smoke? If so, he had found it, but not in the way that he would have liked. He had a terrifying feeling that he was to have an intimate relationship with the fire and the bubbling liquid.

His legs stopped moving, He wasn't going any closer to it.

"No!" he screamed. "I'm not moving."

"Oh yes you are!" bawled a voice behind his head, as a solid object thumped into his back and sent him flying forward, aquaplaning across the shallow water stopping only when he made contact with a roughly hewn floor consisting of a mixture of filthy matting, small stones and shards of broken glass. A luminescent light illuminated the inside of the cavern. Skeletons, missing various bones dangled from the ceiling, hung by their elongated necks in poses that suggested the owners had once suffered great pain; giant cobwebs occupied every nook and cranny; spiders hurried about their business, devouring flies and other invertebrates; wooden shelves were stacked with spell books; glass jars containing repulsive ingredients: bats' wings, frogs' legs, bulls' blood and pickled brains[mincemeat really], adorned a section of the floor in the centre of which stood a huge cauldron, large enough to accommodate a child or two, with a fire burning fiercely beneath it. It contained a bubbling, boiling, lumpy mixture, some of which spilled over the lip.

Andrew looked up and saw a scene he had seen before, but where? Then it dawned on him: this was a scene very similar to the frieze in his classroom. But how? Who was responsible? No, he couldn't believe that Ms Salmon had anything to do with this nightmare, a nightmare that got worse when his vision was confronted by a grotesque face with bulging bloodshot eyes which bored into his soul; a thin pair of lips that were contorted into a malignant sneer and loose flesh that dripped from her jowls, flapping gently, and unpleasantly, in the gentle breeze as she moved her foul head from side to side in the way of a bizarre greeting.

"Welcome to my world," she cackled, pointing to the steaming cauldron that bubbled and crackled.

The horrible realisation that the rumours surrounding the existence of evil witches in the dells on Halloween were true hit Andrew like a sledgehammer. He and his friends had a made a massive mistake, they should never have ventured into the dells on this night of all nights; they should have listened to their teacher and stayed at home. But it was too late now; the woman, Grizelda, raised her arm which held a wand, waved it three times in ever decreasing circles, mumbled something, and the explosion that followed was the last thing Andrew saw!

Satisfied that Andrew's quest was over and a new, horrific, chapter was soon to be written, in blood, Grizelda left the cavern, leaving the goblin to guard the unconscious boy. She headed slowly out of the culvert, across the makeshift bridge, and then up to the main path, a bright light shining from her eyes and smoke billowing from her open mouth. She was looking for the other brats, and she thought she knew where to find them. Soon, very soon, when the clock struck twelve, the so-called Super Sleuths would be unrecognisable and exist no more!

Chapter 10

Jess crawled on to the moss-covered log, that had been made more slippery than normal by the torrential rain that had fallen on the previous few days. The spray coming from the raging torrent, which was normally the slow-moving water of the stream below, made her task much more difficult than usual. She had sprinted across this bridge many times before, but she couldn't do that now, not in the total darkness, and when the surface of the log was covered in slimy, wet moss. She took a deep breath and began her perilous journey along the slightly angled tree trunk knowing one slip and her quest to discover the truth about the mysterious smoke coming from somewhere in the dells would end abruptly. Not only that, a fall of five metres into the rubbish-strewn stream could be much more disastrous than ending the investigation; a fall could threaten her life! With these unpleasant ideas dominating her thoughts, she slowly edged forward on her hands and knees desperately clinging onto the greasy surface, unable to see more than a few centimetres ahead of her, but could hear, despite the noise deadening mist, the crashing of the water below.

Seconds later – it seemed like minutes to Jess – she reached the halfway point of the bridge where a small twig protruded from the trunk at forty-five degrees. She clung to it desperately, her heart racing. Only a few metres to go. Nearly there she thought, a faint smile of satisfaction flashing across her face, but which was almost immediately removed by the sudden and devastating appearance of an apparition standing directly in front of her. It was a creature: a vicious-looking goblin! Shocked, she recoiled in horror and as she did, so her left leg slipped off the log; she screamed and crashed onto the moss-covered surface, sliding inexorably towards the void and a watery grave. In desperation, she flung out an arm, just managing to gain a tenuous grip on the slender branch that was sticking out. The goblin laughed at her perilous predicament and edged towards her, arms outstretched, his evil intentions clear. He was moving closer and closer towards her immobilised body. She panicked. What could she do? How could she escape from this fiend? She couldn't go backwards; she couldn't even stand up to face him; she was barely hanging on to the log and he was much bigger than her anyway. The raging water swirled menacingly below. The goblin slowly bent down, his spidery fingers moving nearer to the hand that was precariously holding onto the twig, which, at the moment, was the only thing stopping her from a lethal descent into the raging current below and, disturbingly, it was bending and creaking under the strain of her weight. Seeing this, a mischievous smile crossed the goblin's hideous features as his fingers brushed against Jess' hand. He was going to dislodge her grip, but she couldn't do anything about it.

She was going to fall into the stream, and it would be all over. She was going to die! As his elongated digits began to curl around her bloodless hand, a voice penetrated the gloom.

"Jess, I'm here. Where are you?"

The interruption startled the goblin. He attempted to stand upright to see through the gloom and identify the source of the voice, but as he did so his left foot slipped off the log. Despite a desperate last-ditch attempt to regain his balance and grab a handhold, his body followed his leg off the bridge and down towards the fast-flowing stream. His screams of anguish were cut short by his heavy landing, in a discarded supermarket trolley that was being bombarded by the cascading water. A combination of the volume of water and the goblin's weight and momentum dislodged the trolley from its resting place and both it and its occupant were transported at speed downstream.

Jess, meanwhile, was still clinging onto the branch, relieved to see her attacker disappear, but not yet safe. How was she going to get off the log? Was that Richard's voice she had heard? Where was he? What was that creature that tried to throw her into the stream? These were the thoughts that rattled through her mind as she felt one of her legs slipping off the tree trunk. With a superhuman effort, she pulled herself up level with the top of the log and with her attached hand threw herself forward, landing heavily on her face, but with a more secure hold on the damp wood. Carefully and slowly, she slithered along the wet surface until she reached the far bank, climbing down from the fallen tree and collapsing, exhausted, onto a pile of leaves.

Chapter 11

On his return from his abortive trip to find Andrew, Richard had sensed that Jess was in difficulties, but he could only hear the sound of the rushing water down in the river bed and could see nothing other than a wall of misty blackness, but he felt something was wrong which is why he had shouted. Dismayed when there was no reply, he was about to climb onto the log and discover the source of his unease and, if she was in trouble, help Jess, but before he could do so a terrifying howling noise assaulted his ears. "Sounds like wolves," he said aloud. "No it couldn't be. There are no wolves in this country," he reassured himself.

The howling noise grew louder; the animals were getting closer. He peered into the gloom for a sign of the creatures that were definitely heading his way. The sounds were louder and more strident. *The sounds of angry animals who sought a victim...* him he thought, looking for an escape route. The log bridge had disappeared from sight; he'd become disorientated. The mist was clouding his vision. Think, he must think of a way to escape from whatever was coming towards him. The howling had turned into growling. He could sense the animals' presence, they were near now, very near. A twig snapped behind him. He automatically moved forward, crashed into an unseen tree, immediately realised its potential as an escape route and began to climb up it using his upper body strength to grab a branch and haul himself off the ground just as two wild animals exploded out of the mist, teeth bared, eyes blazing with malice. They dived at the tree, clawing at the trunk with razor-sharp claws. One scrambled a metre up, gnashing teeth narrowly missing Richard's right leg which he had swung upwards a moment before the jaws snapped shut, but the other had the heel of his trainer gripped in its foul mouth. Clinging onto the branches with his strong arms, he swung his free foot in the direction of the creature's head, connecting with its snout. It immediately released its grip and crashed to the floor pawing its injured nose. Incensed by this attack on its mate, the other hound redoubled its frenzied efforts to savage Richard's dangling body, but by this time, now that his feet were unencumbered, he had climbed rapidly upwards, stopping only when he was safely beyond their reach. Sweat poured from his brow as he gasped with relief.

Once he had recovered his breath, he climbed higher, and the creatures disappeared from view; the snarling stopped. He paused to assess his position and that of his friends. It wasn't looking good for any of them he suspected. Sophie and Kelly were way back in the dells; he hoped they'd decided to go home, but he doubted they had. They were scared and frightened, but they were also brave and determined, despite what they sometimes said. Andrew was lost somewhere on the upper slopes. He was clever and resourceful, armed with plenty of equipment for survival, he should be all right. What about Jess? Had she fallen into the swollen stream, or was someone, or something waiting for her on the other side of the bridge? They were divided and lost, he concluded, and no nearer to finding the source of the smoke, or exploding the rumours about the existence of witches on this night of nights. The whole adventure was turning into a disaster, a Halloween nightmare. But Richard was determined to find his friends and discover who, or what, was behind this mystery. He didn't believe in witchcraft; he felt certain some malevolent character was behind it.

His thoughts were rudely interrupted by a conker which struck his head. He looked around, astonished, to see a group of red squirrels pelting him with missiles. *Strange,* he thought *red squirrels don't live in this area, nor do they hurl conkers at people.*

They then threw some more and bounded off towards the second, or secret, dells. Though he didn't know why, Richard interpreted this as a sign to follow them, hoping it would lead him to his friends, the source of the smoke and a successful end to their investigation. Gathering his strength, he climbed higher up the horse chestnut tree until he found himself on a high-level canopy where the branches were closely intertwined, and he found he could easily crawl along it. The mist was far below, and the crescent moon was shining, illuminating the scene above the trees. Down below he could hear the muffled sounds of hounds yelping in frustration as their prey had escaped their evil clutches. Dismissing them from his thoughts, he followed the squirrels who led the way, occasionally stopping, seemingly, to beckon him on. Richard felt a surge of optimism; things were going to get better he thought, but he was wrong, very wrong!

Suddenly the squirrels disappeared. Richard stopped, mesmerised by the plume of smoke that had risen up from a tree not fifty metres from where he was perched. He was again in a dilemma. Should he climb down from the trees and try to find his friends, they might be danger and he might be able to help, or should he investigate the smoke, that was after all why they were in the dells on this nightmarish night? As he was considering what to do, a swarm of bats flapped past his head; one landed on his neck and started to chew his flesh. He swatted it off, but it was replaced by another and then another. The flying mammals engulfed his head. The decision of what to do next was made for him as he attempted to escape from the attention of the bats by climbing off the canopy and down the tree he was in. As he descended, he held onto the branches with one hand and tried to remove the blood-sucking creatures with the other. The further down he got, the thicker the mist became and the more frenzied the attack by the bats. Blood seeped from his neck where he'd been savaged; he was beginning to feel faint, but he was still only halfway down the tree. He had to reach the ground before he lost consciousness. It was a desperate race against time and gravity. He tried to ignore the bats and use both hands to hold onto branches in an attempt to accelerate his downward momentum away from the voracious mammals, but he found it difficult to grip anything with his blood-soaked hands. He could no longer hold onto the branches; he felt himself slipping, falling. Were the hounds waiting to savage him, he wondered; then he hit the ground, and the lights went out!

He awoke a moment later staring into the rabid eyes of a giant wolf-like dog centimetres away, lips curled, canines exposed, dripping saliva and its foul breath filling his nostrils. Crouching immediately behind the hellhound was the sneering visage of a hooded witch, crimson eyes blazing hatred, thin lips displaying a malicious sneer.

"Comfortable?" she hissed wickedly as she controlled the animal's movements by way of a choker chain, allowing it to move closer to Richard, its snarling intensifying the nearer it got to its intended victim. In a futile attempt to escape, he tried to move backwards, sweat mingling with blood issuing from a cut on his face and neck, but his retreat was halted by the presence of a tree. He was trapped! He tried to raise his arms to defend himself from the attack he knew must be coming, but he couldn't, his arms were securely tied. The hound edged closer, almost smiling, snarling louder. The woman flung back her head and launched into a hideous cackling, looked at Richard and released her hold on the dog. Free from restraint, it bounded forward towards Richard's body, which he could barely move. He made one last desperate effort and succeeded in rolling to one side, just as his canine attacker was in mid-flight. The hound flew over Richard and crashed into the tree that he had been propped up against, yelped pitifully and slunk off disconsolately and grabbed his flailing arms and pulled him back onto solid ground.

"That was brilliant," said Kelly, sarcastically.

"It's wet," he mumbled, in the way of an excuse.

"So are you," laughed Sophie, "in more ways than one!"

Kelly grinned; Scott scowled to mask his embarrassment. "You try standing on the step."

"I'll do better than that," Kelly replied and leapt effortlessly onto the first stone and then proceeded to bound along the next five and would have continued had she not hit a problem.

This came in the form of an overhanging branch which she didn't see, but felt, as her head made painful contact with it causing her vision to explode into a cascade of stars. She would have toppled into the cloying grip of the swamp had it not been for Sophie who had followed leaving Scott to wallow in mud and self-pity. As Kelly's dazed body had begun to waver unsteadily Sophie ed forward and managed to grab her with both hands to steady, and thereby prevent, her from tumbling the mire and a premature, and perhaps, permanent end role in the investigation into the plume of smoke. together, the two girls swayed to and fro on the stones as Sophie held Kelly tightly until she her senses and, more importantly her balance. while, Scott had discarded his self-pity and had show the girls how good his balancing skills re whilst crossing the stepping stones,

into the undergrowth towards the stream, tail hanging between its legs, closely followed by the goblin who grabbed its collar and dragged it back to its mistress.

The witch shrieked in disappointment. "You monster. Look what you've done to my playful pet, Silas. This is another crime you're going to pay a heavy price for."

Richard was barely conscious, but could just see the woman raise an arm which held a stick of some sort. He vaguely heard her mutter some mumbo jumbo, saw a flash of intense light, and remembered nothing else.

"Gag him and drag him to the den," bawled the witch addressing the goblin who was standing nearby clutching the whimpering hound.

He smiled, nodded then attached the rope that was connected to the hound's collar to Richard's bonds. He gave the dog a nudge with his foot to encourage it to move, which it did, dragging the boy's unconscious body along the muddy path towards the gate at the opening of the culvert.

The witch grinned grotesquely and rubbed together her scrawny, flaky hands. It was all going according to the master plan. Nothing could stop them now. Revenge, sweet revenge was on the menu. Midnight was waiting. It wouldn't be long now!

Chapter 12

With the main path blocked by the presence of the witch, Sophie, Kelly and Scott were confronted by a huge dilemma: to try to find their friends, and somehow go back to where they left them, or find their way to the second dells and meet them there.

"What do we do now?" moaned Sophie.

Kelly thought deeply, unusual for her. "We could try getting to the second dells by going through the swamp," she suggested.

"That's dangerous, especially in the dark and this dense mist," said Sophie.

The alternative route to the second dells suggested by Kelly was indeed a perilous one as it involved passing through a stinking, noxious quagmire full of reeds, bits of cars, and, of course, the ubiquitous shopping trolley. The swamp was an effective barrier to those who weren't aware of the existence of a series of small, slippery stepping stones that ran from a spot just off the main path through the dells to the overgrown track that led to the entrance of the culvert, which marked the gateway to the secret dells. All the children knew of the stepping stones and had travelled safely across them many times when they had been playing a game of 'survival' in the dells, but

significantly, only in the daylight; never when visibility was virtually zero.

Nonetheless, Scott was convinced it was the right option.

"It's worth a try and I know the way," he sai confidently. "Follow me."

Reluctantly, seeing no alternative, they did. Min later, Scott had miraculously guided them to the ed the swamp which was obscured by darkness and sh in an eerie mist.

The girls glanced at each other and shudd didn't like the look of this place; something they both sensed an alien presence.

Kelly reacted. "I hate this place, it' muttered, irritably stamping her feet in th beneath her feet and splattering an unin who was about to express her displeasv when she was prevented from do enthusiastic exclamation.

"Look!" he said, kneeling dow flat, slippery object. "It's one of th

The girls stopped glaring at the stone Scott was now h astonished that he had not better still, had located the s hoped, to a reunion with Je

"Look at me," he ord slipped off the wet ston the foul swamp had K

notwithstanding his earlier mishap. He was about to leap onto the first one when a hoarse voice whispered in his ear, "Don't even think about it."

Shocked, Scott's head swivelled round to identify the speaker, expecting to see a friendly face, but didn't! What he saw was a hideous creature with piercing eyes and an evil smirk that stretched from ear to ear. The apparition, a goblin, raised a gnarled hand, topped with long, sharp talons and slowly lowered it towards Scott's paralysed face. Fortunately for him, fear mobilised his body. He turned and jumped in the direction of the swamp and miraculously landed on the first stepping stone. Instinct for survival and panic guided his footsteps from one stone to the next as the sound of heavy breathing and cursing drew closer from the creature that was following him. He was about to redouble his speed when he barged into Sophie and a now conscious Kelly. All three screamed and grasped each other tightly, trying desperately to avoid plunging into the swamp.

"You idiot, now look what you've done!" squealed an angry Sophie, holding onto Kelly, but trying to push Scott away.

"It's coming!" screamed Scott, by way of a hurried explanation for his sudden, and unwelcome contact with the girls.

"What is?" asked Kelly, holding on grimly to Sophie, but seeing nothing in the darkness.

"That is," said Scott, nodding his head in the direction of the dim light that was just visible through the gloom.

The girls looked, screamed, panicked, disentangled themselves from Scott and skipped expertly away from the source of light, remembering to duck under the fallen branch. Unfortunately, Scott was unaware of the bough's existence until he wrapped himself around it before sliding, head first, towards the mire, but was prevented from entering it by a surprising, and unwelcome, source: a large, hairy hand.

"Not yet," its owner screeched. "It's not your time, yet." Saliva dripped from the goblin's open mouth as he spat the words into Scott's terrified face. The goblin then plucked the helpless boy from his precarious resting place on the edge of the stepping stone, applied his foul hands to Scott's exposed neck and began to squeeze.

"This is a foretaste of what's waiting for you in the den," he seethed, as Scott's eyes began to bulge, and his tongue lolled from his gaping mouth as the goblin increased the power of his grip. Sensing Scott's impending demise, the goblin relaxed his grip on the boy's throat, but not out of a sense of pity.

"I don't want you to miss your spectacular finale," he hissed and was about to throw the gasping boy over his shoulder and carry him off when a conker struck his head, closely followed by another and then another, each larger and more painful on impact than the last. The goblin roared in discomfort and looked up towards the top of the overhanging trees trying to catch sight of his assailants, but as he did so one conker struck his left eye. In short order, a second knocked the torch that was loosely tied to his head into the swamp. He staggered backwards clutching his painful eye, tripped over an uneven stone and disappeared into the swamp where he was soon thrashing wildly in an attempt to stop himself from being sucked under the foul water by the weeds and the rubbish that attached themselves to his flailing limbs. As the goblin was falling into the mire Scott slithered from his loosened grip and lay gasping for breath on a small stone.

Observing this as best she could from a safe distance Kelly sensed this was the moment when they could make their escape.

"Quick Scott, follow me," she shouted.

The other two followed her as she leapt expertly from slimy rock to rock with astonishing skill, a talent she didn't realise she possessed. Sophie was more cautious in her movement, being anxious to avoid a disastrous immersion in the swamp. Scott brought up the rear, glancing back every two seconds to see if the goblin was following. He wasn't, he was far too occupied in extricating himself from the foul water, clinging weeds and irate creatures that were unhappy with his presence in their domain.

Suddenly Kelly stopped, almost causing Sophie to crash into her.

"What's wrong?" she asked

"There's two lots of stepping stones," said Kelly, "going in different directions. I can't remember which one leads to the other side and to the path to the secret dells."

"I've no idea either," said Sophie, shrugging her shoulders.

At that moment Scott arrived and announced, "I know which way to go, it's this pathway on the left."

Doubtful, the girls chorused, "Are you sure?"

"Absolutely. Follow me to freedom!" he exclaimed and edged past the cynical Kelly and Sophie and led the way with the girls carefully following him.

Thirty seconds later, Scott had reached the last stepping stone and jumped on to the bank.

"See? We're here. We've made it," he beamed in self-congratulatory mode. "We'll be able to find the others now."

The girls joined him on the side of the swamp. and peered through the gloom.

"We've been here before," announced Kelly, dismissively.

"I know that," laughed Scott. "We've been here lots of times when we play survival."

"She means a few minutes ago," muttered Sophie. "You idiot you've brought us back to where we started."

Scott's jaw dropped as it slowly dawned on him that Sophie was right, and he had made a massive mistake; another. Worse was to come as they could hear something large and angry splashing through the stinking water of the swamp and the sound was getting louder as the creature drew closer. The goblin's cursing assaulting their ears.

"Now look what you've done," hissed Kelly. "More trouble and it's all your fault."

Once more Scott began to regret his involvement in this crazy investigation and started to sob in an attempt to gain some sympathy from the girls. It didn't work, he received only their disgust!

"Follow me," said Kelly, taking the initiative for once. "Not you," she added to Scott. "You can go home," and with that, the girls began to clamber as quickly as they could along the path back to where they first met Scott a few minutes before, conscious of the nearby presence of both the goblin and the witch.

Scott's sobbing ceased with their departure. He sat down, looked around and had no idea what to do next, forgetting about the goblin until he heard watery footsteps sounding much closer and clearly coming towards him. He leapt to his feet and headed in the same direction as Sophie and Kelly. Reuniting with them was his only chance of escaping from this nightmare he decided, or so he thought, but as usual he was wrong, very wrong, as subsequent events were to prove.

"Wait for me," he muttered to himself not wanting to alert the goblin of his position.

Seconds later, the girls heard his clumsy movements and reluctantly stopped to allow him to join them.

"What do we do now?" asked Scott, panicking, and confused.

"We can't go any further up the slope," said Kelly, "because that horrible woman is somewhere up there, looking for us."

"And we can't go back towards the swamp because of the filthy and angry goblin who is also searching for us," added Sophie, shaking, her nerves shot to pieces.

"I know what I'm going to do," said Scott. "I'm going

home." Though he could see very little, he set off running in the direction he thought was home along an indistinct and narrow path that was carpeted with leaves and mud. He didn't get very far.

"He's gone," wailed Sophie, "we're all alone again."

"Good riddance," said Kelly, "he was no use anyway."

"I agree, but what do we do now?" asked Sophie, totally confused.

Kelly was prevented from answering by the arrival of another goblin, crouched on a supermarket trolley that burst out of the darkness in a cloud of spray as the raging stream spat out its unwilling traveller. The trolley hit a rock and the goblin was catapulted out into the darkness beyond the startled girls.

"What, and who, was that?" spluttered Kelly, as she ducked out of the way of the flying trolley which landed upright on its three wheels and rolled back towards the stream where it came to a halt.

"Looks like another goblin and I don't like the look of him either. I don't think he's here to help us," replied Sophie, her fear mounting. "Let's go."

"But where?"

"With me!" screamed a voice in Sophie's ear.

She jumped back in shock, turned and gazed into the grinning creature's hideous face. She collapsed in a heap on the soggy ground. Kelly's blood froze. She was terrified; her legs wouldn't move. The goblin inched towards her, arms outstretched. Suddenly a figure, Scott, flew through the air and crashed into Kelly's attacker, knocking it to the floor. She seized the opportunity and scrambled up the slope, away from the stream and the goblin, slipping and sliding, desperate to escape from the fiendish villain. Her fingers dug into the mud as she tried to ascend the steep, muddy slope.

"Come back," cried a voice out of the darkness.

No way, she thought, finally reaching the relative safety of the leaf-strewn path where she collapsed, gasping for breath. Her head felt to be on the verge of exploding with fear and stress. She slowly sat up, wiped her brow with muddy hands and realised she had escaped.

"Safe," she muttered, feeling relieved.

"Correct, "croaked a voice. "You're safe with me little girl."

Kelly tried to stand up, but her legs had turned to rubber, she sank back to the ground. She was lost and defeated. She'd given up. Something tapped her on the head, followed by a blinding flash and Kelly knew no more.

Down by the stream, Scott was on his knees, mortified by Sophie's condition and dismayed by Kelly's departure. He'd risked life and limb to rescue her, and she'd run away from him. He was about to drag himself to his feet when two strong green hands, with long bony fingers, plucked him off the floor and threw him into the river, launching him downstream where he fought against the strong current. He lost and was carried away shouting for help, desperately flailing his arms in a vain attempt to stop his momentum.

"Bye, bye little man," grinned the goblin, sticking out

a serpent-like tongue between short, sharp fangs. He then scraped Sophie up in his arms and climbed slowly up the slope to the main path to join his friend, the witch who had just relieved Kelly of her interest in the here and now.

Chapter 13

Jess knew nothing of what was happening to her friends. She was recovering from her ordeal on the log, but she was conscious of the passing of time. It was nearing midnight, and that she felt was the crucial time. That was when whatever was going to happen would happen. She peered into the gloom across the bridge looking for Richard as she'd expected him to follow her across the log. *Where is he?*" she wondered. He couldn't have fallen into the stream; he was too strong and resourceful. Something must have happened to him, or perhaps he was trying to rescue the others. That was more likely, she thought. Energised by this she was about to stand up and go back across the bridge when she heard a muffled sound that was getting louder. She could hear leaves and twigs scattering from two directions and they were both heading her way. She realised that a decision had been made for her: she was going to have to return from where she had come from . She took a deep breath; she could see nothing, but could hear deep breathing and guttural sounds. It was now or never. She turned, faced the bridge and launched herself across it, trying to imagine she was crossing in broad daylight, as she had done many times in the past, and pretending that there were no vicious creatures in pursuit trying to do her harm.

She had reached the middle of the log when the snarling hounds erupted out of the darkness howling and gnashing their teeth. They didn't stop when they encountered the log. One after the other, they leapt onto the makeshift bridge, their paws skidding and sliding on the slippery surface in a desperate and forlorn attempt to remain on it so they could savage their prey. Jess carried on running; she couldn't stop now, nor could one of the hounds which made a last desperate lunge at the terrified girl, caught the tail of her coat in its sharp fangs and then tumbled off the bridge, followed a fraction of a second later by its mate. The hem of Jess' coat ripped and disappeared with the hounds in the swirling water while Jess dived onto the bank on the other side, flopping to the floor, physically and mentally drained. Why, oh why, had they decided to investigate the plume of smoke and the curious light? Why hadn't they listened to Ms Salmon's warnings? Jess was tough, but she'd had enough. She wanted to find her friends and go home and tomorrow write the most fantastic, but unbelievable story based on their experiences. Slowly, she dragged herself upright only to be met by the icy glare of a witch, nose twitching, warts oozing pus.

"Welcome to a world of pain," she croaked. "We've been waiting for you to join your obnoxious friends for one last time. We've got a special treat for you." She cackled and raised her right hand in which Jess could see through the gloom held a stick, a wand.

The witch grinned and was about to dispatch Jess to a different world when a conker landed heavily on her already battered beak. She dropped the wand, screamed piteously, and squeezed her nose, trying to stem the flow of blood. As the woman cursed and gesticulated violently at the playful squirrels with her free hand, Jess received the message. She dived into the undergrowth and scampered up the slope towards the relative safety of the playing fields that lined the edge of the dells. Her thinking was that she might see a dog walker, even though it was very late. If she did, she could ask him or her to phone the police and rescue the others. But unfortunately for Jess, and the fate of her friends, she was disorientated and was heading in the wrong direction. She was moving back towards the school grounds, but more importantly, she was on a collision course with the goblin carrying Sophie. Neither of them knew that, not yet!

The goblin was following in the footsteps of the witch, Gizelda, who had tied Kelly's hands behind her back and was pushing her into the mist, the way forward illuminated by a light attached to her crumpled headgear. However, he was struggling to keep up, he wasn't as strong as he thought he was, and the shoulder he had injured in his perilous journey in the trolley was causing him pain.

"You go on," he said, dropping Sophie on the wet ground with a splat. "I'll catch you up."

She snarled, "Weakling!", gave Kelly a kick as though it were her fault and carried on without him, dabbing her bleeding nose with her sleeve and dragging the distressed girl behind her.

The goblin sat down and produced a bottle of beer from his tunic and swigged the lot as Sophie writhed in discomfort on the ground. He needed that; it had been a hard night. He smirked, as he nudged Sophie with his toe.

"Don't worry it'll be all over soon," he said, and threw the bottle over his head towards the stream. It landed heavily on the apex of Scott's head sending him reeling back the way he had come from his unwelcome dip in the freezing water from which he had escaped by accidentally bouncing off a rock and landing on the bank. The ill treatment he had suffered had galvanised him into seeking revenge, though as it turned out that was short-lived. Not knowing the consequences of his antisocial action, the goblin decided he needed a short nap to boost his energy levels before the night's activities began at the witching hour. He closed his eyes and promptly fell fast asleep dreaming about the dreadful things that were going to happen to the horrid brats, who, he was assured, deserved everything that was coming their way.

Seeing her captor was in the land of Nod, Sophie tried to stand and run off, but could only manage to kneel before she fell over and landed uncomfortably in a pool of muddy water. She burst into tears. She wanted to be at home in bed, warm and cosy, not here, wet, cold and frightened. She hated the dells and was terrified of the hideous people she had encountered. Her loud sobs failed to wake the goblin but were sufficiently loud to attract the attention of Jess, who had been stumbling about in the undergrowth nearby.

She recognised the owner of the sob immediately. "Sophie's in trouble," she muttered to herself. She threw caution to the wind and skated down the slippery slope to where she thought the sound came from. She burst through the bushes just as the slumbering goblin was dragging himself unsteadily to his feet, her raised knee striking his jaw before she landed on the floor next to Sophie, who couldn't believe her eyes. Nor could the goblin who was catapulted down the slope towards the stream and the trolley which he miraculously rolled into. Jess jumped to her feet and followed him down the slope to make sure he was out cold. She was delighted to see that he'd finished up in the trolley which, amazingly, was standing upright on its three remaining wheels, seemingly waiting to be launched into the steam. The goblin slowly opened his glazed eyes, looked into Jess' vindictive eyes, felt the cold metal encasing him, looked at the stream and said, "Don't you dare."

Jess ignored his command and launched the trolley, and the goblin, into the current with her foot and waved him goodbye. His screams of, "Mummy help me," surprised, but did not immobilise Jess as she quickly climbed up the slope to untie Sophie with whom she would plan their next move.

"Thanks Jess," she mumbled. "How did you find me?"

"Luck really, but I'm glad I did. I didn't like the look of that creature," replied Jess, relieved that she had got rid of another nasty.

"So can we go home now? I'm tired, wet through and scared."

"Not yet. We need to find the others first and then solve the mystery."

In her misery Sophie had forgotten about the others. "Sorry Jess you're right of course. Where are they?" she stammered. "Have they been captured by some horrible person too?"

"Kelly might have wandered back home, though she wouldn't know her way in this mist; she's probably lost. Richard and Andrew wouldn't have left without us. Besides, they will want to solve the mystery of the smoke more than ever and find out who these ghastly people are that are roaming the dells. They'll not give up, and nor will I."

"Me neither," said Sophie, not entirely convincingly, but she did want to help Jess find the others, and she was especially worried about Kelly. "So where do we go?" she asked.

Jess had decided where their friends must be. "We're going to the second dells, or secret dells as they are often called."

"You mean over the log bridge and through that scary tunnel?" she asked, shaking like a leaf, as she thought the secret dells were terrifying. She'd heard the rumours, and none of them were good.

"We're going to the culvert, but we're not going to use the log bridge, it's too dangerous. We'll use the rope swing further up the dells and nearer to the tunnel to cross the stream."

Sophie gulped, she wasn't good on rope swings, but she'd give it a go as she had no choice.

They stood up ready to go when a hand landed on Sophie's shoulder.

"Got you!" cried the person to whom it belonged. Sophie fainted in shock and fear as Jess picked up a rock; she wasn't going down without a fight.

"No don't hit me, it's me," said Scott holding his bruised head.

Jess dropped he rock, which landed on his foot, and then punched him in the stomach. He collapsed in a heap on the ground and gasped, "Why did you do that?"

"Because you frightened the life out of Sophie. Look at her, you idiot!"

"I didn't mean to scare her. I'm here to help you," he moaned not knowing which part of his anatomy hurt the most, his head where the bottle had hit him, his stomach where Jess had thumped him, or his foot.

Jess doubted he would be any use, but as he was here, she couldn't send him home.

"Okay Scott, no more stupidity. This a dangerous place as I'm sure you are aware. Full of wicked people and vicious creatures."

"I know I've met a few of them," he said, hopping on one leg, clutching his stomach and looking at Jess mischievously, which she saw, but ignored.

Having quickly restored Sophie and restrained her from attacking Scott, Jess led the way up a slope through the mist towards where she thought the rope swing was. The other two followed in single file, Scott reluctantly at the back.

Chapter 14

Despite the mist, lack of light and the muddy ground, Jess moved quickly through the trees and brambles. Sophie and Scott followed closely, neither wanting to be left behind, both pushing and shoving each other trying to avoid being last. A minute later, Jess reached the main path that ran through the middle of the dells. She knew where she was and how to find the rope swing that would enable them to cross the stream without having to confront the perils of the log bridge. Jess didn't want to go there again: too many painful and horrific memories from the recent past. The rope swing, she hoped, would be a much safer option, if it was still there.

"How much further Jess? I'm tired," whispered Sophie, exhausted and frightened. So was Scott, but he didn't say so, preferring bravado.

"I like rope swings, they're fun," he added attempting to sound enthusiastic, but fooling no one.

"If it's still there you'll be fine. It's only a short distance from one side to the other. You've been on it before and you swung across easily," Jess said trying to reassure Sophie.

But she remembered the last time she had a go on a rope swing and still had painful memories of slipping off and spraining an ankle and a wrist.

"Remind me why we need to cross the steam," she asked, utterly confused.

"Because it's our only realistic way to the second dells and that's where the smoke must be coming from."

"What about Richard and Andrew? Where are they?" asked Scott.

"Knowing the boys, I think they'll be way ahead of us and are probably already investigating the secret dells as we speak. They might even already have solved the mystery," she said, believing it to be true.

She couldn't have been more wrong.

Chapter 15

She was right about one thing though, because Andrew, Richard and Kelly had located the source of some smoke, but none of them was in a position to do anything about it as they were all bound, gagged and tied to wooden stakes hammered into the ground in the witches' den staring blankly at a cauldron and its bubbling ingredients. They watched helplessly as two of the vile women, Greta and Grimelda, stirred the foul mixture with a great wooden spoon. One of them filled a ladle and strolled over to the three imprisoned children thrusting it in their faces, threatening to pour the contents on their heads. As she approached Richard, swinging the ladle mockingly, he glared at her. Undeterred by his hostility, she came closer still, her long crooked and bloodied nose centimetres away from him. She snarled and spat venom in his face. He recoiled in horror and then he noticed something strange about the woman's hideous facial skin. It was furrowed and craggy, wart infested, filthy and shiny with an odd lustre. It didn't seem real, even for a witch, She flicked her head to see if her friends were enjoying her performance and as she did, her face seemed to slip slightly.

How could that be? thought Richard, his brain consumed and dulled by the rage he felt inside. Andrew noticed the movement too. The woman's hands shot to her face and appeared to readjust it! She glared hatred at them, re-joined the other women and burst into song: *Hubble bubble toil and trouble fire burn and cauldron bubble!* and cavorted around the cauldron. As they did so, Andrew looked at Richard. They both had the same feeling that there was something odd about this woman. Something was wrong here; the witches were wearing masks! All was not as it seemed. A glimmer of hope surged through both boys. They looked at Kelly who was sobbing quietly. She had not yet recovered from being threatened with the ladle and she had not seen what they had. She was convinced that she wouldn't see her mum and dad, or, more importantly, her dog again. The tears flowed more freely as she fainted away. Richard and Andrew looked at their distraught friend with even greater resolve. They knew these people were not who they seemed to be, which made them more determined to escape and get justice for their suffering, but they didn't know how.

The women's chanting was cut short by the appearance of a goblin, Leonardo, at the entrance to the den who pointed to the clock that was hanging on a wall.

"Nearly time," he announced gravely.

The women stopped singing. They looked at the clock, turned and stared at the three frightened children, walked slowly up to them laughed in their faces and chanted: "It's nearly time. It's nearly the end of your time on this planet as whole human beings!"

The children shuddered as the witches gathered in a

huddle smirking and pointing at their captives, and then held their long, pointed noses, sank to their knees and pretended to drown. Andrew and Richard looked nonplussed. Kelly, now awake, was totally confused. She thought it was a joke at first, then realised where she was and what vision was in front of her, then more tears left her eyes and splashed to the floor.

Grimelda sidled up to Kelly and said, "I've got a special treat for you, my dear. You're the aperitif for the main meal!"

Kelly's face drained of blood and was replaced with a look of panic. She didn't like the sound of that. Nor did the others who made a desperate, but forlorn, attempt to free themselves from their bonds, only succeeding in burning their wrists where the ropes cut viciously into their skin. The witch, who still had blood oozing from her snozz following its earlier repeated contact with numerous conkers, grabbed a petrified Kelly and thrust her forward towards the cauldron; her eyes screamed terror, as the gag prevented her from making a noise. She was about to faint; she'd lost all hope, again!

"No you don't, milady," screeched the witch, "not yet. We want you awake to enjoy your wonderful experience," and dragged the limp girl away from the bubbling cauldron towards another large cooking pot in the corner of the room. This was filled with water, ice cold water. In it floated a number of pieces of fruit, all rotting and maggot infested. "We've got a little snack for you to enjoy, before you become an ingredient in the meal!" she cackled, her face radiating malicious joy at Kelly's mounting panic.

The boys watched on with glazed eyes; they were firmly secured to their stakes and could do nothing to help their doomed friend. They watched as her reluctant body was pushed towards the pot by two pairs of strong and hairy hands until Kelly hovered perilously over the pot, poised to be plunged into the foul mixture. She resisted with all her strength, desperate to keep her face from being thrust into the mire.

"It's called apple bobbing," Grimelda screeched in Kelly's ear.

"It's a traditional fun activity at this time of year," added Greta, laughing dementedly.

Kelly closed her eyes as her gag was ripped from her face. "You won't be needing this," Greta squawked, overcome with the prospect of dunking Kelly's head into the water. Kelly gasped for breath. Which was she going to do first drown, or choke to death?

"Dunk her after the count of three," growled Grimelda. "One, two—"

"Stop!" bawled a voice. "We don't want to spoil her for the banquet to come. Besides Gertie wouldn't be pleased and that would be bad news, very bad news, for all of us," said Grizelda shuddering at the thought of her cousin's notorious anger.

Reluctantly, the other two witches flung a relieved Kelly back towards the stake she was previously tied to. "Your time will come. Soon!" hissed Greta in Kelly's face, as she secured the petrified girl's bonds once more.

The boys smiled with their eyes in an attempt to cheer Kelly up, but failed.

"Right, you two go and find the others," ordered Grizelda. "Leonardo here," pointing to the goblin, "can guard these vile brats in the corner."

"What are you going to do while we're trudging through the dark, muddy dells?" asked Greta, suspiciously.

"I'm going to fetch my cousin and her friend as it's nearly time. So you'd better have captured the others. You know what she's like if people fail her."

They did and shivered involuntarily.

"There's no time to waste," they yelped and scuttled off though the passageway that led to the culvert and the dells.

Grizelda glared at the children who were still firmly secured to the stakes, despite their efforts to free themselves.

"Don't move. I've got a particularly unpleasant surprise for you. Your night is going to become even darker."

That sentiment rang in their befuddled ears while Grizelda left the cavern by a concealed door that led to another route out of the dells. Richard and Andrew renewed their furtive attempts to untie themselves, but with no luck. Leonardo watched their futile efforts and smiled. He knew what was coming, and he relished the thought.

Chapter 16

The doorbell rang, repeatedly, at Cloggham Hall. Gertie stuffed the pork pie she was eating into her mouth almost, but not quite, choking and ambled out of the kitchen hoping the visitor was her cousin.

"Answer the door. Quickly!" bawled Ivan, an extremely unpleasant man with pale skin, one sunken eye, protruding fangs and slicked-back hair. It was Halloween so he was modelling himself on one of his heroes: Dracula! He, like Gertie, was expecting good news just before midnight. He was hoping the person ringing the door bell was the bearer of the information he was waiting for.

Gertie waddled to the great doors, opened them a fraction and peered out into the darkness. Directly in front of her was the panting, sweating form of Mrs Dumpling, dressed as Grizelda.

"It's done," she spluttered. The brats are tied up, petrified and sobbing piteously, wanting their mummies! All they need is for you to finish them off, and we'll all be happy."

Gertie's purple wart throbbed and expanded, doubling in size, as it always did when she was excited, and now she was very excited indeed. The brats who had contrived to escape from the delicious trap that she and Ivan had cooked up for them some months before were now about to get their comeuppance in a very big way. They were going to pay a heavy price for the inconvenience the police put her and Ivan through when they were arrested by detectives Pond and Shunt, the undercover agents acting as their servants at the Hall. They had been accused of child abduction and worse. Fortunately, they had had no case to answer as both policemen, whose testimony was crucial to the case against them, had been compelled to leave the constabulary before they could present a valid case, on the grounds of ill health. This was due to the long-term effects of concussion which they incurred in the line of duty, when they were working at the Hall after they found themselves on the receiving end of numerous 'accidental' beatings. So, this was revenge time for Gertie, and provided the opportunity Ivan had been impatiently waiting for: to transform this particular group of children into the walking dead!

"They're all ready for us in the den in the dells, Gertie shouted to Ivan. "Bound and gagged. Immobile and silent. Just as we like it."

He slammed shut the book he had been reading, *A Hundred and One Ways to Die on Halloween - The rise and rise of the Zombies*, levered himself slowly out of his chair and then leapt in the air in an explosion of joy. He rushed into the hall, grabbed his Dracula cloak and was raring to go. Gertie arrived seconds later, her greasy green locks covering most of her face, but not the monstrosity that constituted her nose, nor could it disguise the wart that

121

was flashing like a warning light. She too was appropriately dressed: long flowing black dress, a capacious cloak, all adorned with a crumpled, pointed hat.

Grizelda, still standing at the door, was suitably impressed by their appearance.

"What a sight!" she exclaimed, slightly ambiguously.

Gertie and Ivan took the remark at face value and perceived it as a compliment.

"Right let's go. Lead the way Grizelda," commanded Ivan as Gertie's mouth was otherwise engaged in eating an extremely sticky toffee apple, which stuck to her lips, cheeks and chins, doing little to enhance her appearance, but plenty to spread her purple lipstick over most of the lower part of her face. After walking a few steps to where Ivan's vintage Bentley was parked, they jumped in and drove to the top of the second dells some two hundred metres away.

On arriving, Ivan clambered out and was following Grizelda to the concealed entrance to the secret tunnel that led to the well-prepared den a short distance away when he realised Gertie was absent.

"Still eating, no doubt," he spat angrily and turned to see where she was. She was still in the car, her face stuck firmly to the dashboard. "Hurry up," he bawled, "we've got villainy to perform at midnight, which is fast approaching."

"I know that you idiot," she muttered in a muffled voice," but I can't move. My face is attached to the toffee apple which is stuck to the dashboard. Help me."

Angrily, he marched up to the car, opened the door

next to where Gertie was sat, and, slapped the back of her head, which broke the seal between toffee apple, her face and the dashboard. Then he viciously yanked her head backwards and said, "There, that's better, isn't it? Now let's finish the job we started all those weeks ago."

Incandescent rage surged through Gertie's veins when her eyes stopped spinning from the blow and she tumbled out of the car, carefully grabbing a cake from the door well before she left.

"This way," giggled Grizelda, foolishly, as Gertie thought she was laughing at her misfortune and never forgot a slight, and never failed to inflict payback with interest, which in this case was immediate, as she pushed the remains of the toffee apple into Grizelda's left ear. Grizelda said nothing; she knew when silence was worth its weight in gold, or in this case, lack of pain. She carefully eased the sticky mush out of her hearing apparatus and tossed it into a bush when Gertie was distracted by the overhanging branches which were disturbing her coiffured hair.

The entrance to the secret passageway leading to the den was narrow and well camouflaged by bushes. Beyond the vegetation was a padlocked gate, which Grizelda had opened on her way to Cloggham Hall. Once they entered the passageway, Gertie snatched the key to the gate off her.

"Give that to me. I'll look after it," she hissed. "You'll probably lose it." She slammed the gate shut and locked it. "We don't want any unwelcome visitors," she added, glaring at her cousin.

The passageway was wet, low and narrow. All three had to crouch down to avoid hitting their heads, with Grizelda poking a finger in her ear trying to remove the last of the toffee apple. Although Grizelda's torch illuminated the way, progress was relatively slow until they heard the unmistakeable sounds of *Hubble bubble, toil and trouble, leg of toad, eye of bull, fill my stomach till its full*, the muffled, anguished cries of the captured children, the crackle of burning wood and the appetising smell of what Gertie liked to call 'child broth'! The ingredients of which consisted of a combination of olive oil, bats' wings, spiders' webs, bulls' eyes, frogs' legs and one special ingredient which still needed to be added: children!

Ivan, closely followed by Gertie, with Grizelda bringing up the rear, burst into the den and glared at the three startled and terrified children. Gizelda ceased chanting, stopped in her tracks and smiled unpleasantly. She was going to enjoy this, but the brats weren't.

Eyes blazing with pent-up fury Gertie waddled over to the children.

"Well, well, well," she seethed. "What do we have here? Three vandals, three thugs who dared to enter my house without paying the price, and also juvenile delinquents who have been a constant thorn in the sides of hard-working and delightful dinner ladies who look after your every need each lunch time and have done for years. And what do they get? Nothing but cheek and bad behaviour from you. You're the worst of the lot. A disgrace to humanity. You don't deserve to be on the planet as human beings, and you won't be for much longer!"

The three captured children looked at each other in disbelief, horror. They couldn't understand how Gertie and Ivan were not only free, but here! The last time they saw the dastardly duo, they were being taken away to the police station to be charged for the evil actions they had attempted to commit against them. But what they did know was that the dire situation they found themselves in was about to become a whole lot worse!

Gizelda was smiling at their obvious discomfort and terror and nodded her agreement with Gertie's sentiments. She was so excited that she grabbed Grizelda's hands and they danced around the cauldron singing *Hubble bubble toil and trouble, leg of toad, eye of bull, fill my stomach till it's full*! Ivan grinned, never a pleasant sight, now more horrible than ever, and was tempted to join them, but didn't. He'd waited for this moment for weeks. Gertie moved slowly towards the children, glaring directly at Richard who glared back, and then at Andrew and Kelly who closed their eyes, not believing what they were seeing, Andrew wanted an explanation and Kelly just wanted to go home. Then Gertie stopped suddenly, and turned to face the witches.

"There's only three here; where are the others?"

The women's joy evaporated.

"Er, only three came," said Grizelda.

"No, there are always five of them. Where are the other two?"

"Oh, now I remember. They're dead. They fell in the stream and drowned," lied Grimelda, sweat destroying her make-up.

"Have they?" Gertie growled, sarcastically, gripping Gizelda by the hair. "Where are the other two brats really, you halfwit?!"

"I think they must have gone home," she squealed as Gertie tossed her onto the floor like a rag doll.

"Where are the other two children?" she shouted at the three terrified women.

"Never mind, their time will come, "interrupted Ivan, livid at the women's incompetence. "We've still got these three to work on," he added, a smile returning to his grim features and saliva dripping off his fangs.

"I suppose so," muttered Gertie eyeing the women with utter contempt. She turned and faced the children again who were still bound and gagged.

"Have nothing to say for yourself, eh? No, I thought not. I'll take your silence as guilt!"

"No lucky escape for you this time," said Ivan, gloating, the pain from the memory of his previous failure to transform the children being quickly forgotten.

Gertie strolled over to the cauldron that was bubbling nicely thanks to the fire burning brightly beneath it. She grabbed a ladle off Grizelda, filled it with the vile mixture that was cooking in the pot and dribbled it into her mouth and down her chins and then spat it out.

"This tastes disgusting," she screamed, castigating the women with her coruscating gaze. "It's missing an essential ingredient: children!" she squawked, walking over to Andrew and grabbing his ear, yanking him closer to the steaming cauldron, so close that the fumes caused his eyes to water and his mind to explode in terror. She pushed him back onto the floor, snarled, selected a large carved pumpkin and placed it carefully on the floor in front of the children. "This is what's going to happen to you miserable creatures," she grinned and stamped heavily on the oversized fruit, smashing it into numerous pieces, several of which struck Grizelda on her already battered nose, causing tears to flow and her make-up to trickle down her face. She was about to complain when Gertie interrupted. "Pick up the pieces and add them to the contents of the cauldron."

"Good idea. Child broth needs some fibre to complement the flesh," she gushed, forgetting the pain as saliva dribbled down her chin, and did as she was commanded.

"Of course it's a good idea, because it's mine!" Gertie shouted, staring at her captive audience and pointing to the pot. "Soon, very soon you'll be joining the pieces of pumpkin!"

The witches cackled with joy and then burst into their favourite chant again, *Hubble bubble toil and trouble...* as they danced round the cauldron. Ivan and Gertie were so overjoyed with the prospect of finally getting revenge on the accursed children that they joined in.

Sweat poured from the furrowed brows of the three petrified children, but it wasn't from the heat of the fire, it was because of the clear, evil intent on the faces of Gertie and Ivan.

"Your time's evaporating like the delicious liquid in the pot," barked Ivan, pausing in his bizarre gyrations to stare at the captives and point menacingly at the clock whose minute hand was perilously close to midnight.

The precious seconds were ticking away, and the children knew it, but were powerless to prevent what seemed inevitable!

Chapter 17

As Gertie and Ivan were becoming not only intimately involved, but taking the lead, in the gruesome events that were taking place in the den on this night of nights, in the dells, Jess led Sophie and Scott, carefully avoiding the slope that formed the shallow, but steep-sided valley containing the stream, to where she thought the rope swing was hanging. It was so dark she couldn't see it, but felt with outstretched arms, attempting to find it through touch. The other two did the same. Sophie was the first to find it.

"I've found it!" she squealed, excited but apprehensive.

"Great," said Jess, relieving her of the rope that was in Sophie's grasp. "I'll go first and see if it's safe."

Sophie nodded, pleased she wasn't going first. Scott was less happy and leaned on a tree waiting for his turn when to his surprise he discovered he was holding another rope.

"Look what I've got," he announced, showing the others. "I'll go first," and with that, he grabbed the rope that he had found, took two steps backwards to give himself some momentum and then ran forward and launched himself into space, gripping the rope as tightly as he could, but immediately noticed something was wrong.

The rope was slippery, very slippery; he was sliding down it and it was making a peculiar hissing sound! How was that possible? It was a rope, or so he thought, but he was wrong, it wasn't, it was a vicious viper! His hands slipped further down the 'rope' until his eyes were level with the end. Imagine his surprise as he was staring at unblinking eyes and a forked tongue; the end of the rope he thought he was holding was not a piece of hemp, but a snake, one that was being elongated by his weight and it wasn't pleased with the result! It hissed and spat at him as the 'rope swing' lost its momentum and Scott continued to slip down. His grip was going; he began to panic. He was going to fall into the rock-strewn stream below and break his legs, or worse, his neck. The snake was no help as it snapped its head back releasing him into the air and he would have crashed painfully into the stream were it not for Jess who had swung herself across the stream on the other rope at the same time as he had to make sure he was safely on the other side.

In mid-flight, she noticed that he was slowly sliding down what she thought was a rope and losing his grip. Sensing his plight when she landed on the far bank she immediately pushed off again, back towards where Scott was dangling so precariously. As she approached him, she grasped her rope more tightly with one hand and grabbed Scott's collar with her other just as his grip failed him.

"Grab my hand, Scott!" she roared as she was having difficulty holding on to his jacket. He flung his hand up and gratefully took hold of her arm. The combination of

Jess' momentum and Scott's weight sent them flying back to where Sophie was standing, almost knocking her over as they landed in a heap.

"Thanks Jess," he spluttered.

"I thought you said you could swing across easily." bawled Sophie, angry that he had endangered Jess by his apparent stupidity.

"I can," he muttered, "on a rope, but not on a snake!"

"A snake!" squealed the girls.

"Yes, a snake. It was attached to the end of the rope."

The girls were stunned. "How has a snake become part of a rope swing?" asked Sophie, baffled and bewildered.

"Not by accident," said Jess, now more determined than ever to cross the stream and solve the mystery. "Somebody is obviously trying to stop us finding the source of the smoke. I don' know why, but I'm going to find out. Come on let's go," and with that, she leapt onto the rope and swung across the valley and then returned the rope to Sophie, who followed with a little help from Scott who gave her a gentle push to give her some extra momentum which would ensure that she reached the other side safely. Scott followed, using the rope, rather than the snake, and had no trouble crossing this time, much to his relief.

As he landed in an untidy heap on the bank near the girls, who slowly moved away from the edge, he turned to see if the snake was visible. If it was, and it was out of striking distance, he'd decided to stick his tongue out at it to demonstrate that he hadn't been afraid of their unscheduled meeting and had won their battle. Disappointed that he could see no sign of the snake, he was about to join the girls when he heard a faint hissing noise. It didn't sound like crashing water, and it appeared to be getting louder. As it sounded ominously like a scaly reptile, one not dissimilar to the one he had encountered minutes before, Scott began to regret his act of bravado and turned towards Jess and Sophie when something lightly flicked his ear. He paused and foolishly tried to brush the cause of the irritation off with his hand, thinking it was a leaf. It wasn't! As the realisation dawned on him that the tickling sensation he could feel on his ear was nothing to do with a tree, but was in fact a flickering tongue belonging to the snake which he had inadvertently upset; he was horrified!

But worse was to follow as something far more substantial and scalier began to encircle his weedy neck. The enraged snake had returned to complete its deadly mission with some style. Scott tried to utter a plea for help, but couldn't as the reptile sought to exact a terrible revenge for the indignity it had suffered earlier when he had elongated its body. The boy clawed manically at the snake's thick coils as they tightened their grip on his neck with ever-increasing force. Scott's breathing became laboured, and he found it difficult to swallow. The blood drained from his face and his eyes bulged to the point of exploding. He desperately wanted to scream for help, but his voice box was being crushed, preventing any sound from emerging from his contorted mouth other than a into the undergrowth towards the stream, tail hanging between its legs, closely followed by the goblin who grabbed its collar and dragged it back to its mistress.

The witch shrieked in disappointment. "You monster. Look what you've done to my playful pet, Silas. This is another crime you're going to pay a heavy price for."

Richard was barely conscious, but could just see the woman raise an arm which held a stick of some sort. He vaguely heard her mutter some mumbo jumbo, saw a flash of intense light, and remembered nothing else.

"Gag him and drag him to the den," bawled the witch addressing the goblin who was standing nearby clutching the whimpering hound.

He smiled, nodded then attached the rope that was connected to the hound's collar to Richard's bonds. He gave the dog a nudge with his foot to encourage it to move, which it did, dragging the boy's unconscious body along the muddy path towards the gate at the opening of the culvert.

The witch grinned grotesquely and rubbed together her scrawny, flaky hands. It was all going according to the master plan. Nothing could stop them now. Revenge, sweet revenge was on the menu. Midnight was waiting. It wouldn't be long now!

Chapter 12

With the main path blocked by the presence of the witch, Sophie, Kelly and Scott were confronted by a huge dilemma: to try to find their friends, and somehow go back to where they left them, or find their way to the second dells and meet them there.

"What do we do now?" moaned Sophie.

Kelly thought deeply, unusual for her. "We could try getting to the second dells by going through the swamp," she suggested.

"That's dangerous, especially in the dark and this dense mist," said Sophie.

The alternative route to the second dells suggested by Kelly was indeed a perilous one as it involved passing through a stinking, noxious quagmire full of reeds, bits of cars, and, of course, the ubiquitous shopping trolley. The swamp was an effective barrier to those who weren't aware of the existence of a series of small, slippery stepping stones that ran from a spot just off the main path through the dells to the overgrown track that led to the entrance of the culvert, which marked the gateway to the secret dells. All the children knew of the stepping stones and had travelled safely across them many times when they had been playing a game of 'survival' in the dells, but significantly, only in the daylight; never when visibility was virtually zero.

Nonetheless, Scott was convinced it was the right option.

"It's worth a try and I know the way," he said confidently. "Follow me."

Reluctantly, seeing no alternative, they did. Minutes later, Scott had miraculously guided them to the edge of the swamp which was obscured by darkness and shrouded in an eerie mist.

The girls glanced at each other and shuddered; they didn't like the look of this place; something felt wrong; they both sensed an alien presence.

Kelly reacted. "I hate this place, it's scary," she muttered, irritably stamping her feet in the muddy water beneath her feet and splattering an unimpressed Sophie, who was about to express her displeasure in strong terms when she was prevented from doing so by Scott's enthusiastic exclamation.

"Look!" he said, kneeling down and touching a small, flat, slippery object. "It's one of the stepping stones."

The girls stopped glaring at one another and looked at the stone Scott was now balancing on. They were astonished that he had not only found the swamp but, better still, had located the stepping stones, the path, they hoped, to a reunion with Jess, Richard and Andrew.

"Look at me," he ordered moments before his left foot slipped off the wet stone and he would have tumbled into the foul swamp had Kelly and Sophie not reacted quickly and grabbed his flailing arms and pulled him back onto solid ground.

"That was brilliant," said Kelly, sarcastically.

"It's wet," he mumbled, in the way of an excuse.

"So are you," laughed Sophie, "in more ways than one!"

Kelly grinned; Scott scowled to mask his embarrassment. "You try standing on the step."

"I'll do better than that," Kelly replied and leapt effortlessly onto the first stone and then proceeded to bound along the next five and would have continued had she not hit a problem.

This came in the form of an overhanging branch which she didn't see, but felt, as her head made painful contact with it causing her vision to explode into a cascade of stars. She would have toppled into the cloying grip of the swamp had it not been for Sophie who had followed her, leaving Scott to wallow in mud and self-pity. As Kelly's dazed body had begun to waver unsteadily Sophie leaned forward and managed to grab her with both hands trying to steady, and thereby prevent, her from tumbling into the mire and a premature, and perhaps, permanent end to her role in the investigation into the plume of smoke. . Locked together, the two girls swayed to and fro on the slippery stones as Sophie held Kelly tightly until she regained her senses and, more importantly her balance.

Meanwhile, Scott had discarded his self-pity and had decided to show the girls how good his balancing skills really were whilst crossing the stepping stones, strangulated gurgle. As the snake's mouth opened wider and wider, a terrified Scott was able to observe not only the creature's throat, but its empty stomach, which he had an uncomfortable feeling he was about to fill!

The reptile's beady eyes glowed with pleasure as it revelled in the fear that radiated from Scott's optics. Now satisfied that its mouth was open wide enough to engorge half of Scott's head, the serpent arched its neck preparing to strike with its vice-like jaws when it felt the unmistakeable presence of five strong digits gripping its tail. As it attempted to swivel its head to face its new adversary it was yanked forcibly off Scott's enfeebled body by a powerful and angry Jess who had a firm grip on its scaly skin. She swung the befuddled reptile around her head as though she was throwing a hammer. She rotated on her heels three times and then released her grip on the snake and launched it across the stream where it landed on the far bank with a splat, quickly slithering off into the undergrowth to lick its wounded pride. Jess then scraped the gasping Scott off the ground with one hand and gently slapped his face with the other to make sure he was awake, and his mind was fully focused on their real task.

"Thanks," he mumbled, not knowing which to rub first his neck or his cheek. "I think."

Sophie doubted it in the light of his actions.

Jess ignored Scott's bleating, intent on finding their friends, solving the puzzle of the smoke and discovering the source of the mysterious and sinister creatures they were encountering.

"The culvert's this way," she said, hurriedly heading towards where she thought the metal gate was that usually blocked access to the large cylindrical pipe beyond it which led to the secret dells. Although Scott had not fully recovered from his close encounter with the snake, he and Sophie followed closely, nervous, but excited as they thought, mistakenly, they might be nearing the end of their quest.

Chapter 18

Unknown to all the occupants of the dells, another group of costumed people had been secreted in the woods well before midnight. They had been there prepared for moments like this. As far as they could they had been monitoring developments ready to intervene when the nefarious activities of the 'witches' endangered the group of children. The onlookers wanted to know how far the women were prepared to go in their pursuit of misguided revenge, but knew nothing of the malevolent presence of Gertie and Ivan. The watchers were none other than the children's teacher, Ms Salmon, three of her teaching colleagues and Mr Williams, the school's head, who had nervously agreed to help his intrepid staff to prevent potential trauma and injury, or worse, to some of his pupils. They were in the dells because Ms Salmon had overheard the dinner ladies finalising their plans on the school drive after school had finished, when she had been waiting for a child to be picked up by a parent running late. She had explained the situation to Mr Williams and outlined what she thought was the best way of dealing with it. He had agreed that action must be taken to stop the women from implementing their wicked plan, and wanted to do something about it immediately. Ms Salmon had to use all her powers of persuasion to get him to wait before he intervened and instead accompany her, and the other teachers, into the dells for a midnight rendezvous with the nasty women who clearly had malice in their hearts. She stressed the need to catch them in the act.

By the time the children had arrived, blundering their way through the dells, the teachers, dressed in witches' clothes themselves, were hidden in the undergrowth, watching events unfold and they had a secret weapon, a drone, with a night camera attached, which Mr Williams was operating, enabling them to see much of what was happening in most parts of the dells, but, crucially, not all.

The teachers also had night-lens binoculars, unlike the children's, which enabled them to see even more of the action than the drone could provide, but again, not everything. The dells covered a large area and not all of the teachers knew about the secret hiding places, caves and passageways. They also had to be careful not to be seen, but still be able to observe what was happening. They had to catch the women in the act, but before any lasting damage could be done to the children. This was proving to be more difficult than they had imagined due to the dense mist and the amount of area to be covered. They considered splitting up to follow the various groups, but quickly abandoned that idea as some of the teachers didn't know their way around the dells well enough and might become lost themselves, so they continued to monitor events from their hidey-hole.

Chapter 19

Carefully, Jess threaded her way through the mist-shrouded bushes; there were fewer brambles here, but more saplings and the larger trees were closer together. Their progress was slow, but Jess was sure they were heading in the direction of the culvert and was now convinced that that would prove to be the portal that would lead them to the source of the mystery. She paused to make sure the other two were still with her. They weren't! She heard the clank of a metal gate closing followed by the snap of a twig, the crunch of leaves, voices, horrible croaky voices; she ducked down. Where were they? She couldn't speak because whoever had emerged from behind the gate that led to the culvert was heading towards where she was hiding. A torch partially illuminated the scene, though the mist rendered visibility limited and indistinct. She buried herself under the leaves and could feel something slither up next to her. The snake! It touched her leg; she pulled away from the reptile and felt around for a stick to remove it when a voice whispered. "It's me Jess." The voice belonged to Sophie who had heard the noise before Jess did and had dived to the ground, afraid to speak.

Scott was nowhere to be seen. He too had heard the noise, but had decided to run away. He was heading up the slope to where the teachers were secreted, though he didn't know that. They saw him coming. Should they stop him and let him into their secret they wondered, but the decision was made for them as the witches had heard his dash for freedom, shone their powerful torch in his direction and briefly illuminated the back of his mud splattered head. They cursed violently when they spotted him, hitched up their skirts and attempted to follow him, hoping he would lose his footing, which he did, almost immediately, knocking himself senseless on a rock.

Greta and Grimelda, the witches, advanced towards him.

"One more down, only one to go," they muttered gleefully.

Higher up the slope, the teachers observed events as well as they could through their night binoculars and the drone that Mr Williams was controlling. They were increasingly worried about the fate of the children. Mr Williams, in particular, was particularly keen to intervene, but as Ms Salmon reminded him they had to catch the women in an act of villainy in order to punish them in some appropriate way, depending on what the women had attempted to inflict on the children. Their immediate concern was Scott who they could see was in difficulties as the excited witches scampered over to where the boy's prostrate body lay in the damp leaves. Despite his difficulties, the teachers decided it wasn't the right time to intervene. They would wait a little longer.

The women peered at Scott's face and arrived at the

same disappointing conclusion.

"This is not one of them," said Greta, flummoxed.

"What shall we do with him?" asked Grimelda.

Greta scratched her greasy head with her long purple nails, deftly removing a layer of her make-up, exposing a patch of pale skin that contrasted with the green that enveloped the rest of her face.

"Roll him down the hill, then we'll drag him into the tunnel to join the rest. He'll be a bonus for Grizelda's cousin. I'm sure she'll be pleased with an additional victim."

Grimelda agreed and the two women bent down, rolled Scott into a makeshift ball and booted him down the slope. He went crashing through the undergrowth, narrowly missing Jess and Sophie who had remained hidden during the brief chase. The women followed Scott's path, picked him up from where he had come to a halt, and carried him the short distance to the entrance of the culvert and launched him into the water like a torpedo, his momentum stopped only by the foot of Leonardo who had heard the laughing and cackling of Grimelda and Greta, and the sound of something splashing in the water and had thus been alerted to the likelihood of another victim.

Scott's involuntary immersion in the water had both cleared his nostrils and woken him up, but contact with the large wooden spoon that Leonardo applied to his head, as he attempted to stand, scrambled his senses completely. He didn't know where he was, and he no longer cared! Leonardo bound and gagged him and dragged him towards his friends in the den, though he was sure they wouldn't be mates for long as he had a good idea what Gertie had planned for them, and it didn't involve a long-term friendship!

Meanwhile the women had returned to the undergrowth, near to where the girls were hiding.

"I don't think he was alone," said Grimelda, parting the branches of the nearby bushes and examining the ground underneath.

"No, I think you're right. I'm sure I can detect the stench of frightened children," said Greta, bursting into a hideous cackling that petrified Jess and Sophie who were concealed under a pile of leaves a metre away from the women's feet.

"You go down the hill towards the stream and have a look there. I'll climb up the slope," said Grimelda, kicking the leaves in frustration as she edged towards the girls who were shaking with fear.

"When I get my hands on them they'll wish they'd never been born," she growled, moving still closer to the nervous girls. She peered into the gloom, but could see nothing. "No sign of the other brats."

"Must have sneaked off home, blubbering, wanting their mummies," sniggered Greta.

"Let's go back to the den and enjoy the forthcoming entertainment."

"Yes, see our captives beg for forgiveness—not that they'll get any from Grizelda, and definitely not from Gertie, or Ivan!"

Jess and Sophie, only a few metres away from the

gloating witches were appalled to learn that the others had been captured and taken to some sort of den where someone called Gertie was involved. Surely not Gertie Grimbody they thought! If it was that would be very bad news indeed as they knew what she was capable of from old. She loathed Jess and her friends and was capable of anything. But they dismissed the notion, it couldn't be her she was in jail, or should be.

"Come on, let's go before we miss the fun and games," urged Greta.

The witches had a last look into the darkness, saw only mist, even though the girls were within touching distance and headed towards the culvert.

"We can't just stay here, we have got to do something," whispered Jess when she thought the witches had gone.

"You're right. Let's go home and phone the police," suggested Sophie, getting to her feet and preparing to run out of the dells.

"We can't do that. It will be too late to save Richard and the others from whatever these evil people are planning to do. We've got to do something now!" Jess insisted, desperately trying to think of a way of distracting the witches and then rushing into the den and freeing the others.

Sophie was in a dilemma; she wanted to run, but knew she must stay and help Jess.

The clanging of the gate opening focused their attention. They now knew where the passageway was that led to the den, or whatever it was, and they knew it was very close.

"Come on follow me," commanded Jess as she slithered forward across the wet earth, closely followed by a reluctant Sophie.

"What are we going to do?" she asked.

Jess said nothing until they reached the gate, which a quick check revealed was unlocked.

"I have an idea," she said. "I'm going to swing on the gate, so it crashes into the post. The sound it makes will echo down the passageway and with luck they'll think it's us and then, hopefully, they will dash out and try to catch us."

"What do *I* do?" asked Sophie, not understanding the plan, or more specifically her part in it.

"When they appear at the entrance here, you'll be up the slope, out of sight. I suggest you climb up a tree. I'm sure the squirrels will help you," she joked, trying to mask her frayed emotions.

"Then what?"

"You scream and they'll all come looking for you, but won't find you of course. I'll be hiding by the side of the gate. When they've gone past, I'll sneak into the tunnel and rescue Richard and the others," she said not really believing her plan would work, but she had to try something.

"Sounds dangerous to me," observed Sophie. "Perhaps we should—"

Before she could finish her sentence, the sound of feet splashing in the water that trickled though the passageway turned their blood to ice. Watery footsteps and loud, angry voices were heading towards them. The girls could see a faint smudge of light in the gloom of the passageway growing ever larger as it neared them.

"Time to go," begged Sophie.

But Jess was mesmerised not only by the oncoming light, but by her failure to rescue her friends.

"Just forget the plan, let's go" hissed Sophie, her limbs turning to jelly as she attempted to drag a reluctant Jess away from the gate.

Realising her plan was doomed to failure, Jess reluctantly followed Sophie and sprinted through the mist back up the slope towards the dense undergrowth. As the girls disappeared into the darkness, Grimelda and Greta had reached the gate; they had heard whispered voices whose volume had been magnified by the acoustics of the tunnel.

"It was them. I know it was," screamed Greta as they emerged jubilant from the passageway and into a darkness partially illuminated by their now feeble head torches.

"You're right, it was. I'd know their horrible, weaselly voices anywhere," muttered Grimelda. "Come back, you vermin. We've set up a Halloween party and you're the guests of honour," she cackled, as both witches advanced slowly up the slope towards where the girls were now hiding under one of the many rhododendron bushes, where they had scooped together a pile of leaves and covered themselves completely. As the ponderous footsteps advanced towards them, Sophie developed an overwhelming desire to sneeze. She was finding it difficult to stop herself from giving their position away as their enemies were closing in on them.

"Come out, come out wherever you are. We won't hurt you; we just want to take you to a party," lied Grimelda.

Seeing that Sophie's nasal problems were about to explode, Jess thrust her hand over her friend's nose, thereby nipping the problem in the bud, and resolved to leap out if the witches came any closer and push them towards the stream. Then she would run towards the rope swing and escape with Sophie out of the dells, forget the smoke and contact the police. Greta did take a step closer, and Jess was about to react when she was stopped by a thunderous cackling voice which boomed out from above them.

"Stop where you are. Stay still and you will not be harmed!"

The girls cowered in terror. "Oh no, not more horrors. What now?" mumbled Jess, head in hands, on the verge of tears. Even she'd had enough. Sophie was inconsolable.

But the message had not only affected the girls, but it also had a devastating effect on the two witches. Grimelda was immobilised, as was Greta.

"What on earth was that? she wailed.

"It sounded… witchlike," mumbled Greta, beginning to think they might not be the only witches in the dells.

Suddenly terrified, it dawned on them that their nefarious intentions had been discovered by someone, or by something, perhaps supernatural! Both panicked and dashed towards the culvert. The door was locked. Grimelda took the key out of her pocket and inserted it in the lock. It wouldn't turn! She pulled it out and it slipped from her nervous fingers.

"Hurry, they're coming to get us!" screamed Greta, as the sound of bodies crashing through the undergrowth towards them grew louder.

Grimelda plucked the key from its resting place in the mud and tried the lock again. It clicked open. She threw the door back, picked up her long skirt and staggered down the drainage pipe closely followed by Greta.

Further back in the bushes, Jess and Sophie had been astonished by how the events had unfolded. Where had the voice come from? Were they being rescued, or attacked? What was happening? Suddenly, out of nowhere appeared four more witches and what looked like a zombie! Were they dreaming? If they were they hoped that they were good witches. The newcomers swept past the girls and ran towards the culvert. Three of them entered, but one stopped and turned round to face the bemused, terrified girls. Sophie shivered and prepared herself to run off, somewhere, anywhere. Jess prepared herself for action; she wasn't going down without a fight, but before either girl could launch into their different strategies, the witch removed her mask to reveal the friendly face of Ms Salmon! They couldn't believe what they were seeing. Was it really their teacher? Were they now safe? Ms Salmon smiled, waved and then followed the other witches. The girls collapsed, tears of joy flowing down their happy faces.

Chapter 20

Meanwhile in the den Andrew and Kelly were petrified; what was the evil Gertie going to do to them? She looked capable of anything and made the other two women look inoffensive, almost benevolent, by comparison. Richard was anxious, but more angry than frightened. He looked at Gertie, Ivan and the other women, who were all pointing at the bubbling cauldron, then looked at the clock, on which the second hand was on its last circuit before the clock would strike twelve. They guffawed and rubbed their foul hands together, and he feared the worst. Time was running out, but he wasn't going to allow himself to be a victim of their malice; he would come up with a plan, but he needed it quickly! Time was ticking; midnight was fast approaching, then Gertie announced, "Time's up! "

The children shuddered.

"Right, you're first into the pot," smirked Ivan, picking up a wooden spoon, saliva dripping from his fangs, as he and Gertie advanced towards the squirming Richard, hands outstretched, wickedness writ large on their vile faces.

"I'm going to use this utensil to scrape out what little brain lurks inside your vacuous skull and add the contents to this delicious concoction," Ivan snarled, as he stirred the noxious liquid in the cauldron, his one crimson eye glowing with pleasure at the thought.

"Do it. Do it!" urged Gertie, bouncing up and down, unable to contain her excitement.

Before he did, they both averted their scrutiny of Richard's tense face and looked at the scarecrow, a creature with dead eyes and a ghostly pallor that was dangling, tightly attached by a noose, to a beam.

"A zombie!" they chimed, and then stared intently into Richard's appalled eyes.

"You're about to join an exclusive club," barked Ivan, his head rocking dementedly from side to side.

The moment had come for Richard; it was now or never, he thought. But before he could mobilise his strength for one last effort, and just as Ivan's slimy fingers were about to clutch his swaying head and apply the spoon, Grimelda and Greta – who had dashed as quickly as their stumpy legs would allow through the passageway from the culvert – burst into the den screaming, "They're coming to get us. We've been rumbled!"

Ivan's digits froze a centimetre above Richard's hair. "What!" he shouted, hands suddenly limp, the spoon sliding from his enfeebled grasp.

"Who? How? Where?"

"Them. Here. Now!"

Ivan didn't like the sound of 'them'. Thoughts of his unpleasant encounter with the police and the time he spent under arrest alarmed him. But of course it wasn't his fault that they were about to be raided.

"What have you done, you buffoons," he bawled, empty fingers still hovering over his Richard's head.

"Where are they!" screamed Gertie, angry, but worried; she too didn't fancy a return to the confines of a cell, and worse, prison food!

"Just behind us, in the passageway," Grimelda gulped.

Gertie looked at Ivan with fear in her eyes. She nodded, swiftly picked up a heavy ladle and swung it, in the way of a parting shot, at Richard, who ducked just in time, and it missed him by a whisker. But such was the viciousness of Gertie's attack that the momentum carried her through 270 degrees, only stopping when the makeshift weapon hit Grizelda and Gizelda, who were instantly rendered immobile by the contact, knocking them both out cold.

The sound of feet splashing through the water in the culvert galvanised Gertie into survival mode. She stepped on the supine bodies of the two unwilling recipients of her assault, pushed Grimelda and Greta aside and hurried a still stunned Ivan towards the secret passageway leading to where their car was parked. Before she entered the tunnel, she turned and glared at Richard and the others.

"We'll be back. We've got unfinished business," she snarled.

Ivan glared at Richard and pointed to the hanging zombie.

"Don't worry that will soon be what you look like." Both then dashed, surprisingly quickly, up the passageway and out of sight.

Relief at seeing Gertie and Ivan vanish was short-lived for Richard and Andrew as they became aware of the sound of the splashing footsteps moving quickly in the passageway towards them. "Oh no, not more witches," stammered Andrew, fighting back the nausea he felt inside at the prospect of facing more menacing figures.

Richard steeled himself for further resistance. Whatever was thrown at him he was determined to survive. Revenge would be his for all the indignities he and his friends had suffered.

Scott looked at Kelly and mumbled forlornly, suspecting a short future, "I'm sorry I was such a pain."

"It doesn't matter anymore, we're finished," replied Kelly, as the clock finally struck midnight and the new coven of witches burst into the den to be greeted by an astonishing sight. A cauldron was bubbling and boiling in the centre of the den; four children were bound and gagged in a corner, each tied to a stake, struggling desperately to free themselves; two witches were lying on the floor unconscious, blood oozing from a wound on the head of one of them. The other two, who had arrived only moments before and were still reeling from Gertie's push, fainted when they saw their nemesis. What they didn't see was a goblin sneak out behind them and vanish into the culvert emerging into the dells, where he blundered into Jess and Sophie whose smiles disappeared on seeing the hideous creature.

"Out of my way," he bawled as ran past them, slipped

in the mud and slid effortlessly towards the stream.

In the den the witches who had just arrived were relieved to see that no harm had come to the children and smiled at each other. The four captives couldn't believe their eyes: more evil people determined to do them harm? Suddenly a creature appeared that looked like a zombie to the terrified children. It *was* a zombie! It had leathery orange skin, black sunken eyes, a gaping mouth populated by four uneven, sharp teeth and a hole where its nose should be. The whole ghastly face was framed by lank, straggly hair that partially covered pointed, blood-stained ears. It paused, pushed aside the witches, looked around, spotted Andrew and lurched towards him, grinning hideously, thrusting a four-fingered hand towards the boy's eyes! Andrew's heart sank; were these real, or were they imposters, wearing masks too? Was he going to be transformed into a version of the living dead as Ivan had predicted, after all? He soon found out, but not before panic overcame him. He couldn't breathe; he couldn't swallow; he was on the verge of choking when the claw struck, ripping off Andrew's gag with one hand and with the other removing his own mask to reveal the astonishing sight of Mr Williams' worried, but kind face. None of the children could believe their eyes.

"Relax, you're safe now," Mr Williams said gently, beginning to remove the other children's gags and some of the bindings. "I hope I didn't frighten you too badly with my disguise. I wore it, of course to scare these people," pointing to the unconscious witches on the floor.

"You did a bit, but that doesn't matter now. Thank goodness you're here," said Kelly, weeping with relief.

Having recovered from the shock of the appearance of friends rather than enemies and found his voice, Andrew asked, "What are you doing here? How did you know where we'd be?"

"How did you get here?" added Richard, uncomprehending.

"Answers later, let's completely untie you first," which he did with the help of the other teachers. Once freed, Richard and Andrew shook his hand, Kelly's legs collapsed, and Scott burst into tears.

One of the newcomers removed her mask to reveal the face of a beaming Ms Salmon.

They gasped with relief and dashed over to hug their friends. The nightmare seemed to be over.

The children then looked at each other sheepishly.

"We're sorry Miss; we didn't take your advice and stay away from the dells on Halloween," said Andrew.

She smiled. "I'm sure it's not normally like this, but I'm afraid you inadvertently upset some very nasty people," she replied pointing to the unconscious women. "And they hatched a diabolical plan to get revenge, which fortunately for you, I overheard, and with the help of Mr Williams, decided to do something about it."

"Thank goodness for that," said Andrew.

"But we've done nothing wrong," complained Kelly.

Baffled, Richard asked, "But who are they?"

"I think I know who they are," said Andrew.

"Who?" asked Kelly and Scott, in harmony for once.

Ms Salmon removed the mask from one of the women and wiped some make-up off her face to reveal... Mrs Dumpling.

"It's the dinner ladies!" they all shouted just as Jess and Sophie appeared, tentatively, at the extraordinary scene.

"Welcome girls, come on in," said Mr Williams, brightly.

The two astonished girls stood motionless at the entrance, rubbing their eyes in disbelief. They didn't know whether to laugh or cry until they saw the jubilation on their friends' faces and smiled broadly. Then all six children came together and hugged each other in relief. The teachers looked on delighted that they had saved their pupils from further distress, though not realising that the two principal villains had vanished, or the full extent of the wickedness that Gertie and Ivan had intended to inflict on their hapless victims.

"But what are they doing here?" asked Jess, disentangling herself from her friends, pointing at the bedraggled dinner ladies.

"We knew they were unpleasant people, but we didn't know they were capable of such malicious behaviour," observed Andrew, staring with disgust at the heap of semi-conscious women who were moaning and groaning on the floor.

"Why us?" whimpered Kelly.

"What's going to happen to them?" asked Sophie.

As Mr Williams was about to answer their questions, Ms Salmon gave the children a wink followed by a smile. Richard, Andrew and Jess responded by looking at each other knowingly and nodded. They understood that their teacher had a plan. Not seeing Ms Salmon's intervention, and sensing an unhelpful frustration creeping into their questions, Mr Williams decided it was time to draw a line under the night's terrifying activities.

"Don't worry, we'll question them and find out why they lured you into this mystifyingly elaborate trap. The most important thing is that you don't need to be frightened any more. You're all quite safe now. It's very late, just gone midnight. And not surprisingly, considering the horrific experiences you have been subjected to, you're all exhausted so we are going to get you out of here and back to your homes."

The children nodded reluctantly; they *were* all very tired, but wanted to know how their teachers had known about their quest, which without the teachers' help, they realised could have ended disastrously. Ignoring their desperate pleas for more information, the other three teachers guided them out of the dells, using their torches and night glasses. They put the children in their cars and took them   home. All the children had keys with them so were able to let themselves quietly into their houses, being careful not to wake their parents. They climbed into their beds exhausted and fell asleep quickly, the horrors of the night forgotten for now.

In the dells, Mr Williams said, "When I can get a

signal I'll phone the police to deal with this gruesome lot," pointing at the pile of demoralised witches/dinner ladies who were looking very sorry for themselves.

"No need to do that. I've got a better idea," said Ms Salmon. "After all they've not actually harmed the children, though they appear to have wanted to. But my plan will stop them from doing that ever again," she added.

Mr Williams was doubtful, but had confidence in Ms Salmon. He stood back and watched as she produced a torch and a large fob watch from the rucksack she was carrying and proceeded to hypnotise all four of the dazed women and instructed them how they were going to react to a given sign.

The two teachers then led them up to the road at the top of the dells. Once there Ms Salmon snapped her fingers, and they awoke remembering nothing of their nefarious activities in the dells as the teacher had planted in their brains an entirely different scenario to explain why they were dressed as witches. Whilst under her influence she convinced them that they had been to a particularly exhausting Halloween party and were now wandering home slightly confused as a result of the wine they had drunk.

Mr Williams gave Ms Salmon a nod of approval and they went their separate ways, confident that they had resolved the situation in a way that satisfied all parties, but knew nothing of the involvement of Gertie and Ivan whose night had deviated considerably from their original plan

Meanwhile, up in the secret passage, Gertie and Ivan

were dashing up the slope as fast as their unfit bodies would allow them, gasping and panting when they eventually reached the gate. They quickly unlocked it and staggered to their car. Ivan collapsed on the steering wheel, exhausted and angry.

"Your cousin's an idiot," he gasped, still desperately short of breath, but still full of venom. "This fiasco is all her fault."

"Of course it is. Our plan for revenge, and theirs, was perfect, spoiled by a fool. She'll pay for that, just you wait and see."

Ivan had no doubt and relished the thought. Distracted and appalled by Grizelda's incompetence and their failure to finish the children off by transforming them into zombies, he turned the key in the ignition, slammed the car into the wrong gear, stamped on the accelerator in a fit of pique, and promptly shot backwards into a sturdy tree, destroying the boot and giving both driver and passenger whiplash and two black eyes, as their heads collided painfully with the windscreen; then their lights went out!

Chapter 21

The day after their traumatic experience in the dells the 'Super Sleuths', minus Scott, who was still in bed, arrived at school early and were already writing their story of Horror in the Dells when Ms Salmon entered the classroom. Unlike the rest of the class who were amazed to see their friends writing with such enthusiasm, Ms Salmon merely smiled. She understood only too well what they were writing: a story based on reality, with characters that were all too real! They were centred on finding the source of a mysterious plume of smoke and a battle with hostile creatures and wicked witches. After Ms Salmon had given them a few reminders about what she expected to read in their stories, the rest of the class began writing furiously, all keen to put their ideas down on paper.

Just before dinner time, Ms Salmon asked if anyone would like to read out their story to the rest of the class. Andrew volunteered. The class were entranced by his detailed description of the dells and the hideous characters that lurked in it, but most of all the wickedness of the witches. They wondered how he could possibly write so well, as the story seemed real!

He announced, with an enigmatic smile, "I just closed my eyes and imagined it all."

Before he could read out the final chapter, the bell rang for dinner time. Ms Salmon told the class that Andrew could read the ending to them after lunch. The class were disappointed they wanted to know what happened to the story's heroes: the children. So too did Andrew, who felt the real story was not yet over.

After leaving the classroom, Richard, Andrew, Jess, Kelly and Sophie sat together on a bench overlooking the dell reflecting on what Ms Salmon had told them about overhearing the diabolical plans of the dinner ladies; the horrendous reappearance of Gertie and Ivan, and the terrifying events of the previous night. Unlike then the sun was now shining, the birds were singing, their friends were playing games in the yard and on the field all around them and they were relaxed, free from the physical horrors of their Halloween adventure and having seemingly discovered the source of the mysterious plume of smoke, but not quite over the mental trauma.

They all now understood the involvement of the vindictive dinner ladies, and Jess and Sophie now knew about the horrific presence of Gertie and Ivan, as their old enemies had escaped by the time the two girls had arrived in the den. They weren't sorry to have missed them!

"Well that's that then. Mystery solved," said Sophie. "The dinner ladies were responsible for the plume of smoke. Not really a mystery at all. And they should be sacked!"

"And don't forget Gertie and Ivan," added Kelly, shuddering at the mere mention of their names.

"None of them have been punished. Incredibly, the dinner ladies are still here, pretending to do a job," said Andrew, exasperated.

"The teachers don't even know about Ivan and Gertie. Are they going to get away with their horrible actions too?" asked Jess, enraged at the potential injustice.

"Good question and I wouldn't be surprised if they were the diabolical brains behind the whole nightmarish experience," observed Richard, perceptively.

"What can we do about them?" wailed Sophie.

"Nothing, yet. We can't prove anything," added Richard, disconsolately. "We'll just have to watch out for them."

Kelly shuddered as the horrific experiences Gertie and Ivan had subjected her to swamped her mind.

"Let's hope that nearly getting caught has made them think again about hurting people," suggested Andrew, trying to calm his friends' emotions.

"I doubt that very much," said Richard. "They need to be subjected to something truly horrific for them to change their wicked ways."

"They should be imprisoned, for years," demanded Jess, unwilling to forgive what they had made her friends suffer.

"I agree," said Andrew. "They deserve to be punished, but their involvement doesn't explain some of the things that happened in the dells. For example, I don't understand how the squirrels which, strangely, were red seemed to be on our side, bombarding the witches with conkers. The

158

dinner ladies, or Ivan and Gertie, couldn't be responsible for them."

"Yes, the squirrels seemed almost human," added Sophie, "and on our side."

"And what about the bats," mused Richard, as he touched his savaged neck, but could feel no pain or sign of bites, and he wasn't a zombie!

"Except," said Andrew, in the realm of the supernatural…"

"What do you mean?" asked Kelly, suddenly frightened. She didn't like the sound of real witches; false ones were bad enough.

"He means there might really be a magical presence in the dells on Halloween! "observed Jess.

The possibility of real witches, with real magic briefly flickered through their minds.

"No they don't exist, except in the realms of fiction," concluded Andrew. "There must be a simple explanation for the behaviour of the squirrels and bats."

The rest nodded, not entirely convinced; doubts remained.

Behind them the four dinner ladies were huddled together scowling at all the children, barking orders and shouting at a few who dared to be too happy. They reserved their deepest dislike for the five sitting on the bench gazing at the dells, a place they had high hopes for, but which, in the end, let them down badly, though they didn't know why, or remember anything about the Halloween party they had apparently attended.

The five children were unaware of the dinner ladies' presence as they were still reliving their horrific experiences and realising how easily it could have gone very badly wrong were it not for the intervention of their teachers. They fixed their gaze on the skyline where the uppermost reaches were dominated by the denuded branches of the beech and horse chestnut trees, reflecting on the previous night's events, when a singular plume of smoke emerged and formed a hand, which seemed to not only point, but beckon them.

"That's not possible," murmured Andrew, Jess and Richard at the same time, as an icy shiver rippled down their spines.

Then a hand landed on Kelly's shoulder. She leapt forward and screamed in terror. Sophie screamed too, though she didn't know why. Richard, Andrew and Jess all swivelled round expecting to see either a real witch, or a dinner lady, accusing them of some minor misdemeanour, but it wasn't either, it was Ms Salmon, who looked at them, looked at the plume and whispered, "Remember what I said about the dells at Halloween?"

"We remember!" exclaimed Kelly, not wanting to be reminded.

"How could we forget?" added Sophie, trembling slightly.

Understanding their discomfort Ms Salmon said, "Come with me. I want you to see something I think you will enjoy."

Puzzled, but intrigued, they followed their teacher

into the dining hall where the first sitting was in progress, being policed by Mrs Dumpling, Mrs Onion, Mrs Salad and Mrs Sour. On seeing their least favourite children and their obnoxious teacher, they shouted and screamed at random children for either eating their food, or not eating their food, whichever was most inappropriate! Ms Salmon and her five pupils looked at the diner ladies with the contempt they deserved; the women glared at the teacher and were about to continue to berate the diners when Ms Salmon clapped her hands. Everybody froze as Mr Williams appeared with a pair of cymbals which he clashed together twice in quick succession. All the children in the dining hall were stunned. Mr Williams never did anything like that. What was happening? They soon found out.

The four dinner ladies, who had been hypnotised in the dells by Ms Salmon to react to the clash of cymbals, reverted to being witches and began to chant *Hubble bubble toil and trouble, leg of toad and eyes of bull, fill my stomach till it's full, as I go my legs feel wonky, that's because I'm a stupid donkey, hee haw, hee haw!* And gyrated around an empty dining table, stirring the contents of an imaginary cauldron, faces contorted into a grotesque sneer, voices cackling as the words gushed out of their thin-lipped mouths. They cavorted round and round until they were dizzy, crashed into each other and collapsed in an untidy heap on the floor, puffing and panting, much to the amusement of the assembled children. Mr Williams clashed the cymbals again and the dinner ladies suddenly became aware of their bizarre and undignified position in a pile of tangled limbs. They were speechless as Mr Williams approached them, mobile phone in his hand.

"Well ladies, that was entertaining."

The dining hall was in uproar, children laughing and cheering. The women were baffled, they weren't aware of what they had been doing.

"What do you mean?" asked Mrs Dumpling, echoing the thoughts of her colleagues, all puzzled and deeply embarrassed by the raucous laughter all around them, which seemed to be directed at them and based on what they had done.

"Why I mean your ridiculous impression of witches dancing and chanting round a cauldron."

The dinner ladies remembered nothing of their performance.

"He's mad!" screeched Mrs Sour.

"They're all insane," shouted Mrs Dumpling, looking round at all the children who were happy that she and her unpleasant friends were finally getting their comeuppance.

"Calm down, ladies. Look at this video and you'll understand the pleasure you have, for once, created in this dining hall."

He showed them the footage of their performance. They did and didn't like what they saw. Feeling totally humiliated, they looked at each other, grimaced, nodded and stumbled out of the hall as quickly as they could to the accompaniment of thunderous applause from children and teachers alike. Mrs Dumpling stopped at the entrance doorway and announced loudly, "We won't be coming back to this... this hellhole!" she bawled.

"I know you won't," replied Mr Williams, much to the amusement of the staff and the other helpful dinner ladies, who were glad to see the back of what they'd always called the band of witches!

"Well that's the last we'll see of them," smiled Sophie.

"Good riddance," added Kelly, continuing to wave goodbye even though they were out of sight.

Chapter 22

Following the dining hall entertainment and the exit of the four fiendish dinner ladies, a more relaxed Richard, Andrew, Jess and Sophie ate a leisurely dinner at one of the tables whilst Kelly scoffed hers quickly and returned to their favourite bench on the school field overlooking the dells to see if the plume of smoke was still there. It was! She closed her eyes to make it disappear, but she was so tired following her hectic late night she began to daydream.

Minutes later, she was awake. She thought she heard a series of ear-piercing screams coming from the direction of the plume of smoke, which had suddenly disappeared, and the screaming had stopped. Or had she imagined it?

As Kelly had been drifting off, Mrs Dumpling was walking swiftly along the road towards her house. Initially, she had been resentful about the humiliation she had suffered in the dining hall, but the further she walked the more she thought about her actions and began to see the error of her ways—well, some of them. Her journey took her past the gate to the secret passageway that led to the witches' den. As she approached it, the bushes that normally hid it were pushed aside and she could see that the padlock was dangling from the gate in an unlocked state.

"That passageway leads to a dangerous place," she said aloud. "I wouldn't want children to go down there. I'll lock it." Which she did with the key she'd used the night before. "There, nobody will be able to enter now and be harmed," she continued, benevolently.

Though she wasn't aware of the consequences of her actions, of much greater significance was the fact that no one could leave the tunnel. Mrs Dumpling wandered off smiling for the first time for many weeks, having done her good deed for the day. She was a changed woman, but didn't know why.

Prior to Mrs Dumpling's actions, wearing uncomfortable neck braces and dark glasses to disguise their black eyes, Gertie and Ivan had returned to the den, determined to put right the wrongs they had repeatedly suffered at the hands of those horrendous brats.

"We'll light the fire and recreate the mysterious plume of smoke," announced Ivan, as he watched Gertie eat a cake with one hand and stoke the fire with the other.

"That will get the brats down here again and I will succeed in turning them all, every last one of them, into zombies if it's the last thing I do," Ivan shouted in a voice so loud that it not only startled the colony of vampire bats from their sleeping positions, but made them angry, and when they were annoyed they became hungry. This was more bad news for the two villains. The bats immediately swarmed and attacked Ivan and Gertie who both squealed in terror as the bloodsuckers sank their sharp little teeth into any flesh they could find, and there was plenty on offer! Nightmarish visions of being transformed into zombies flooded their minds.

"Quick! To the passageway!" shouted Ivan, panicking, but Gertie had beaten him to it and was already making her ponderous way up the tunnel and soon reached the gate to find to her horror that it was firmly locked. Ivan arrived seconds later, immediately followed by the voracious bats. The pairs' screams of agony disturbed Kelly's daydream.

A hand touched Kelly's shoulder. She shuddered and stared at Sophie.

"Come on Kelly, wake up or you'll miss the exciting conclusion of Andrew's story.

"I already know how it ends. If only!" smiled Kelly and skipped after Sophie with a spring in her step; as she did so she glanced over her shoulder for a last look at the dells to see if the plume of smoke had returned; it had, but had changed its shape. It seemed to Kelly to resemble a squirrel's tail and appeared to be waving goodbye! She waved back and vanished into the school to join her friends, happy, but utterly baffled!